EMERALD HEART

LEIGH STEPHENS

Editors: Carol Nichols, Steve Voyak
Cover design: Chris Lorenzen
Copyright © 2016 Leigh Stephens

ISBN: 0692813578
ISBN 13: 9780692813577

The Old West is not a certain place in a certain time, it's a state of mind. It's whatever you want it to be.

--- Tom Mix, early western film actor ---

TABLE OF CONTENTS

CHAPTER 1

THE TRIP WEST

Nevada 1875

Elizabeth Rogers shoved her elbow into the man's side as hard as she could. His snoring momentarily ceased as he snorted and mumbled incoherently. She breathed a disgusted sigh and poked him again and then pushed him off her shoulder. It had been this way since Salt Lake and she had enough.

The man opened his eyes and looked around at the other passengers on the stage and then focused on Elizabeth, realizing at last that he had once again been sleeping on her shoulder. "My apologies miss," he said in a not-so apologetic voice. "It's difficult to get comfortable when the stage is rocking back and forth." He scooted his body over toward the gentleman on the other side of him who rolled his eyes and leaned as far away as he could.

She did not answer but instead looked out the window and stared. The passing landscape was soothing, and she closed her eyes for a moment thinking of the long way she'd come. Her trip began in Missouri where she grew up on a farm with her parents and older brother Jim. He was ten years older and took charge of the farm and her welfare after their parents died in a cholera epidemic. They worked the land together. Jim spent his days in the fields and she took care of the home while still going to school. He insisted she continue her education.

When the war started, so many boys from their county joined the fight that Jim felt it was his duty to go. His regiment left for Tennessee to face the Confederates and a year later she received a letter informing her that he had been killed. The news was devastating.

Elizabeth opened her eyes when the stage jumped as it hit a rut in the road throwing the passengers into the air then slamming them back down on the hard, wooden seats. The man sitting beside her threw his arm out to catch his balance and slapped her in the face, knocking her hat sideways and crushing the brim.

"My apologies once again," he said as he righted himself. "I believe this is the most uncomfortable ride I've ever taken. Six passengers in a small coach is entirely unacceptable in my opinion."

"It's a tight squeeze that's for sure," said the gentleman sitting on the other side. "And nearly impossible when you insist on lying on top of this young lady and me as you sleep."

"I beg your pardon," said the man indignantly as he straightened the suit jacket stretched over his bulging stomach. "I have every right to rest my eyes during this trip."

"Well, we have every right to sit in peace without listening to your snoring like a grunting hog but that doesn't seem to be the case."

The other passengers joined in the conversation with a flurry of barbs for each other as they aired their grievances. There were accusations of shin kicking, foot stomping, hip nuzzling and foul odors that lasted for the next mile until Elizabeth thought she might just open the door and jump or at least ask the driver at the next stop if she could sit up top with him. Finally, a well-dressed man sitting across from her pulled out his gun and threatened to shoot the next person who opened their mouth with a complaint. The coach fell silent as passengers leered at the gentleman and he put away his gun, pulling out a small cigar instead. He lit the end and leaned back as the puffs of smoke floated out the window. The smell of cigar smoke in such a tight space wasn't the solution Elizabeth was looking for but at least it was peaceful. She stared out the window and thought of home again.

It was impossible for her to run the ranch by herself after Jim was killed so, for a time, she lived with her aunt and uncle. They did their best to include her in their family of six, but Elizabeth missed the house she grew up in. The loss of her parents and brother was overwhelming and when her sorrow was too much to bear, her comfort came from sitting on the bank of the creek near their farm with her feet emerged in the cool running water. As a young girl, she would spend a long summer's day sticking her toes in the muddy bottom while Jim caught crawdads with his makeshift net. The old creek, with its dark swirling water, was a haven and she smiled, remembering those sweet moments of her childhood.

Alex Rogers, like Jim, fought in the war. Upon returning home, he needed employment and found it through working for Elizabeth's uncle on her farm. They met for the first time one afternoon when she sat on the banks of the little creek. He came to fish and forget the things he saw on the battlefield and she, to grieve the loss of her family.

He was a gentle man and a hard worker. Although, not especially handsome, he possessed a quick wit and the ability to make Elizabeth laugh so it was easy for her to fall in love. She wondered now if it was a love that would have sustained but he filled that empty void in her heart and she offered him the home he was looking for. They were married, and Elizabeth was sure she was destined to be happy after all. Fate, however, is sometimes cruel and just when she thought her dreams had come true, her life was torn apart once more.

Their first winter was harsh. Elizabeth couldn't remember ever seeing so much snow. The cold winds would whip over the barren fields and seemed to penetrate every seam in the walls of their home. They struggled to keep the animals fed and watered and Alex wondered if their supply of food and firewood would last until spring. Warm weather arrived, and planting season promised a good year ahead. The melting snows brought surging water and the river, with its swift moving current, swelled and spilled over into the fields.

"Next stop in ten minutes," the stage coach driver shouted down. Passengers began to wiggle in their seats and the stout man next to her tried to stretch his leg but withdrew it when the cowboy across from him cleared his throat and scowled. The gentleman with the cigar sent another puff of smoke into the air and smiled at her. She returned the smile then looked out the window again hoping to see the station in the distance.

Alex would have hated the west. He was a farm boy at heart and loved working the land and raising their stock. They were missing a calf, as she remembered. It rained for three days straight and the roads were all but washed out. Still, he wanted to go despite her worry over the danger. He needed to find that calf. The river was rising over the banks and the poor animal had gotten tangled up in brush wrapped around a fallen tree. Alex worked to free him and as he was carrying the calf up the bank to safety, he slipped and fell back into the water where the rapid undercurrent pulled him down and carried him away. Elizabeth was grief stricken. She shut herself away from everything, never leaving her house. She no longer found pleasure in her childhood home and knew she must leave the lonely place it had become. She decided to sell her farm and move far enough away to forget her sorrow and with the help of her uncle, settled on Nevada as a destination.

"The station is just ahead folks. We'll change horses and then be on our way," the driver yelled down to the coach. Elizabeth straightened her hat as best she could and waited for the stage to stop. The station master, who was a scraggly old man, opened the door and the gentleman with the cigar climbed out first then turned to offer Elizabeth his hand.

"Thank you," she said and climbed down catching the hem of her dress on the stair and tearing a portion. She gave out a dejected sigh and reached to pull it free.

"Let me get that for you," said the gentleman. He reached down and unhooked the hem from the rusty nail it was attached to. "I'm afraid it might have ruined your dress."

Elizabeth gave him a faint smile and walked into the station which was nothing more than a small cabin. It was musty inside and barely lit with a few small windows but there was a table and some chairs and the offer of a glass of water for the passengers. A meal of beans and cornbread along with hot coffee could be purchased for a dollar but after the dusty trip she had no appetite and no desire to sit so she walked outside to watch the station master change the team for the next leg of the journey.

"We should be in town by supper, if all goes well."

Elizabeth turned to see the gentleman with the cigar standing beside her. He looked to be in his late thirties and well dressed for this part of the country. He was slender with smooth dark hair and a thin mustache. She could tell his suit was expensive and he spoke with a slight drawl making him seem out of place in these parts. She was suspicious of a man like him who would attempt to befriend a young woman traveling alone and took a step backwards.

"If all goes well? I don't know how it can get much worse," Elizabeth said. "An entire day spent on this rocking, wooden box, squeezed in next to an oversized man who uses me for a pillow."

The gentleman laughed out loud with such force that it caused Elizabeth to laugh too and her distorted hat slid down the side of her head. "I was wrong," she chuckled. "My new hat is now completely ruined." She straightened it again then looked questioningly at the man. "What did you mean, if all goes well?"

"I just meant we should be on time if we don't run into trouble along the way," he said as he threw down his cigar butt and smashed it into the ground. "These roads are full of ruts and we might lose a wheel. I don't mean to scare you, but stages have been known to be robbed from time to time and there is an occasional Indian attack although I believe those have subsided drastically."

"Well, you've certainly done a good job of not scaring me," Elizabeth said sarcastically. "When does the frightening information start?"

The gentleman laughed again. "I apologize, miss," he said. "It was my intention to begin a simple conversation with the hope of passing the time and now it seems I've blundered the whole thing. Forgive me for mentioning any possible issues we may have on the last part of our journey. I have faith in the Overland Company and know that it will bring us safely to our desired destination."

Elizabeth gave him a skeptical look and thought the best course of action would be to go back to the station house until time to leave and she started to walk away.

"My name is Jack Devlin and I mean you no harm. It's just that, as you say, we've been stuck in the wooden box for many hours and I thought I might introduce myself."

"Elizabeth Rogers," she replied. "Nice to meet you, Mr. Devlin and thank you for quieting down the others during the squabbling, although your method was somewhat unusual." She smiled at the thought of the stunned passengers when he flashed his pistol.

"I have to admit they all made their point, but I wasn't about to listen to them for the rest of the trip. It's amazing how people seem to change their attitude when they're looking at the barrel end of a gun. I hope it didn't frighten you."

"Not at all, Mr. Devlin," she smiled. "I rather enjoyed it and it gave me some peace and quiet which is something I could use right now."

"Where do you come from, Miss Rogers? How is it that a young lady as pretty as you is traveling alone?"

"I'm from Missouri...just west of St. Louis. My husband and I owned a farm there," Elizabeth replied.

"And he is minding the farm in Missouri while you travel west?"

"He was drowned several years ago in an accident," Elizabeth replied, looking away for a moment and pausing. "I'm traveling alone."

"My apologies for prying," replied Devlin. "I'm sorry for your loss. It's been a long trip for you, I'm sure."

Elizabeth took a deep breath. "It seems like it's lasted forever. I left St. Louis last week on the train for Kansas City and on to Omaha from there. Then four nights on the Union Pacific to Utah. I picked up the stage in Salt Lake. How about you, Mr. Devlin? Where did you come from?"

"I can claim a lot of places, Mrs. Rogers," said Devlin. "Most recently Denver where I was participating in a card game which lasted longer than I expected. I'm on my way to Sacramento now."

"To play in another game?"

"It is my profession and I'm very good at it. I've taken this stage because I need to make a brief stop to pick up a horse I've purchased. I'll be taking him west with me."

"Loading up," shouted the station master.

Elizabeth and Jack Devlin headed toward the stage and waited as the other passengers boarded. He held the door as she placed her foot on the stair, mindful of the rusty nail sticking out on the bottom of the step. She turned to Devlin with a serious look. "There aren't really Indian attacks, are there?"

"No, Mrs. Rogers," he smiled. "Not today." He helped her into the coach and waited for her to sit before climbing in and closing the door.

CHAPTER 2

CONFRONTATION

"**Whoa**," **the driver** called as the stage came to a halt. He climbed down and paused for a moment to stretch before opening the door of the coach. "End of the line for the day, folks. You can wait inside if you want while we unpack the luggage. The hotel is down the street to your left and Elkhorn Saloon to your right."

Jack Devlin climbed down and looked around while the station master helped Elizabeth. "Careful of the step," Devlin reminded her and she held up her dress and petticoat to avoid the nail.

Elizabeth watched the chaos on the sidewalk in front of the station depot. A man scrambled to the top of the stagecoach and untied the rope which held the luggage in place while another stood below ready to receive the trunks and carpetbags. Some of the passengers were already inside but the large man who sat beside her stayed and gave directives for his things to be unloaded first.

"What are your plans now, Mrs. Rogers?" said Devlin over the noise. "May I assist in finding someone to help with your things?"

A large mail bag thrown to the ground almost landed on Elizabeth. She scooted out of the way with a frightened look. Her hat began to slide, and she grabbed it with one hand, pushing it back while moving closer to Devlin. She was just about to speak when a cowboy walked up beside her and shouted to the man on top of the coach.

"You got a saddle up there for the Emerald ranch? Suppose to be coming from Denver."

Elizabeth gave the man a disapproving look as she put her hand over her ear to shield it from his shouting. She inched toward Devlin and paused when she heard the tearing of fabric. Looking down, she realized the cowboy was standing on the frayed hem of her dress.

"Got it right here," the man on top yelled back. He picked up a saddle and threw it down to the cowboy who shouted back his thanks.

"Please, sir," she said in frustration as she tried to pull her dress from under the man's boot.

"What?" answered the cowboy. He turned around holding the saddle and knocked her into Jack's arms. "Sorry, ma'am," he said, then hurriedly walked over to the front of the building and dropped the saddle. "I'm going to leave this here for my brother," he shouted to the man on top who was struggling with a large trunk. "He should be here with the wagon in a couple of minutes to pick it up. I've got some place else I need to be."

"I'll see that he gets it," said the station master walking up from behind and slapping the cowboy on his back. "How's that boss man at the Emerald getting along?"

"Barking orders as usual," said the cowboy with a smile. "He's gone and bought his already spoiled daughter a new saddle and sent me to pick it up. I'm running in eight different directions."

"Well, that's why he has you, Matthew," said the station master with a grin. "You and Griffin both work hard for him as well you should. Tell him to stop by and see me the next time he's in town and I'll buy him a drink."

"I will," laughed the cowboy. "Remind Griff when he shows up that I'll meet him at the Elkhorn. I need to run."

"I can't believe..." Elizabeth said to Devlin after she composed herself. Still red-faced, she smoothed her skirt and surveyed the damage to the hem. "I'm sorry that dusty cowhand rushed off before I had the opportunity to tell him what I think. Is everyone that rude in this part of the country?"

"Mostly the younger ones," Devlin said with a grin. "Some of those cowboys spend so much time with their cows they forget how to act around people. They're better off limiting their conversations to animals. Now, as I was saying, would you allow me to have your things removed to the hotel? I'll be staying there myself for the evening and it's no trouble."

"Oh, no thank you," Elizabeth replied. "I'm not staying at the hotel. Someone is meeting me here and taking me directly to my ranch. It's what I've come for. I sold our farm after my husband died and with the help of my generous uncle who has done everything possible to make up for the sadness in my life, I have the money to buy a ranch"

"Ranch?" said Devlin with a look of surprise. "I salute you madam on such a large undertaking for a woman alone. Do you know much about ranching?"

"Not a thing," Elizabeth laughed. "But I was raised on a farm. I know about animals and crops. How much different can a herd of cows be? My uncle insisted I hire a foreman to run things and I plan to learn from him."

"Your uncle sounds like a smart man and I salute him as well for taking such good care of you. Should I wait with you until someone arrives? I have nothing to do until tomorrow when I pick up my horse."

"You're such a kind man, Mr. Devlin. Nothing like the others I've seen so far. I'll be fine by myself. I plan to go inside and wire my uncle that I've arrived safely and I'm sure my contact will be here shortly. Much luck with your next card game in Sacramento and your new horse."

Well then," said Devlin as he reached in his vest pocket and pulled out a card, handing it to Elizabeth. "I can be reached at this address. Please contact me should you ever need assistance of any kind." He smiled as he put the card in her hand. "Should you need a sleeping gentleman forcibly removed from your shoulder or a wild cowboy cured of his rudeness, I will always be at your service."

Elizabeth smiled and said goodbye then walked inside to find the station master. She was anxious to let her uncle know about the trip. She also wanted to find his friend, Will Spencer, who would take her to the ranch. Her spirits were high considering the day she had. She looked frightful with a dress full of wrinkles and a torn hem. The cowboy had knocked one of the combs lose in her hair which was dirty and now in danger of coming completely undone and falling to her shoulders in a tangled mess. She looked forward to a good supper and relaxing bath. Stepping up to the counter, she gave the station master her name.

"Are you Elizabeth Rogers from Missouri?" the station master asked when she inquired about Will Spencer. "He sent over a message saying he's been tied up and asked for you to meet him at his office if that was possible. It's just down the street next to the bank. I can have someone escort you."

"That's not necessary, I'll find it myself." This was a little disappointing, Elizabeth thought as she let out a sigh. She was hoping to leave for the ranch right away and now it seems Mr. Spencer scheduled an appointment. Well, it probably couldn't be helped. After all, a man like Will Spencer had a business to run. The walk would do her good after sitting for such a long time on the stage and she headed down the street.

Will Spencer was a friend of Elizabeth's uncle. They met years ago in St. Louis at the stock yards. Will was a financier and her uncle sold his cattle at the yards. They seemed to hit it off from the beginning and both prospered from the friendship. Will married his wife, Margaret, and moved west in the 1850's during the gold rush. He wasn't interested in prospecting. He had come to invest and settled in Nevada where silver was discovered almost daily.

When Elizabeth made the decision to move west her uncle was frantic. How could a 23-year-old, unmarried woman travel across the country by herself? She would have no one to care for her. It was dangerous and completely unacceptable in her uncle's opinion. But Elizabeth made up her mind and didn't care what anyone else thought.

Out of desperation he wrote to his old friend and asked for help. Will felt honored by the request. He and Margaret set about finding a ranch suitable for Elizabeth. She wanted something with acreage to raise crops and cattle.

He hired the best ranch foreman he could find and stocked the ranch with enough cattle to get started. Repairs were made on the house and buildings which looked run down. Margaret took charge of the furnishings, a job she thoroughly enjoyed and made sure Elizabeth's new home would be comfortable. It was the general opinion of everyone, except Elizabeth, that she would give up the idea of owning a cattle ranch after spending some time in the rough land of Nevada, but Will and Margaret intended to make sure she had everything she needed on this end to be a success.

The door to Will Spencer's office opened with a jolt just as Elizabeth reached for the handle and the cowboy stepped through the thresh hold looking backward as he talked to someone inside.

"Let me talk to Pa about your idea for that silver mine. He may want to include Henry Richter in this deal. I'll stop back later in the week."

He turned around to face forward and not noticing Elizabeth, slammed into her, knocking her backwards with full force. She gave out a yelp and grabbed for his arms to keep from falling as her pitiful hat slid down her head once more.

"Whoa, excuse me miss. I didn't see you there," said the cowboy as he put his hands around her waist to steady her balance and looked down, wondering why her face was familiar."

Elizabeth tore the hat from her head and glared. "You again," she shouted. "Have you no shame? It's obvious you have no manners from the way you acted at the station but now, to push your way through the door like a bull headed for the feeding trough is practically uncivilized. First you push me and tear my dress and now you've stomped on my foot. Hopefully I won't go lame." She winced as she wiggled her toes inside her shoe to make sure they were all in working order.

"Tore your dress?" Matt Kelly said doubtfully, still trying to figure out where he had seen this woman before. "This was just an accident and I said I was sorry. There's no need to get ugly."

"Ugly, now I'm ugly?" Elizabeth screeched in a high-pitched voice. "What kind of thing is that to say to a lady?"

The cowboy shook his head in exasperation. "Look Miss, I'm not calling anyone ugly." He looked around the busy street, embarrassed about the confrontation. "I didn't see you when I walked out, and I've apologized for it. Now you're raising your voice and carrying on..." He paused for a moment as he looked at a pair of pretty, blue eyes giving him a cold stare. She was a little thing, barely came to his shoulder. No wonder he didn't see her. He smiled to himself as he noticed her blonde hair loosely pinned up with something poking haphazardly from her head. What was on the end of the hairpin, a butterfly?

Elizabeth's face turned red with anger. This was the most aggravating man she had ever met. He did, indeed, push her and tear her dress and step on her foot which was hurting now, and he couldn't understand why she was upset.

"Sir," she began. "And I question my judgment in using that term. I am hot and tired and can't remember the last time I've had a decent meal." Tears began to well in her eyes and her voice cracked as she took a deep breath and spoke. "It's obvious you have no sense. Mr. Devlin was right. You just need to go talk to your cows." She threw her dilapidated hat at the cowboy hitting him in the face. "Now if you'll please step aside, I'm late for an appointment."

Matt turned sideways as she squeezed through the door and walked away in a huff. He bent down and picked up the crumpled straw hat decorated with blue ribbons and straightened the bent brim, then headed down the street. What just went on there, he wondered? It's been a busy day and all he did was open a door and walk out. A woman runs into him or, on second thought, he might have run into her. It was difficult to remember with those bright blue eyes staring like you just cussed in church. Hadn't he apologized? Yes sir, he had and still, she threw a fit. Where did she come from? Did she need help? She said she hadn't eaten.

"Well if that's not a sight to behold. The pride of the Kelly family walking down the street muttering to himself." Matt stopped in front of the Elkhorn Saloon and looked up to see his brother Griffin leaning against the side of the building. "Where have you been?"

"I just came from my meeting with Will and he wants Pa to buy into that silver mine."

"What was your answer?" Griffin asked as he pushed the door of the saloon open and walked inside looking for an empty table.

"I told her I was sorry. What else could I say?" answered Matt as the two sat down and motioned for one of the working girls to bring them a couple of beers.

Griffin stared at his brother as if he'd just walked into the wrong conversation. "Told who you were sorry? Where did you say you were?"

"I was coming out of Will's office and ran into a woman," Matt replied. "I may have stepped on her foot, but I did not rip her dress. I'm not taking the blame for that one."

Griffin sat back in his chair and grinned. His brother was completely flustered, and he was enjoying every minute of it. "So, you stepped on some woman's foot, ripped her dress, and then apologized? What about the silver mine?"

"I said we'd think about it and then she told me to go talk to my cows," Matt answered as he contemplated the conversation he had with the woman.

The saloon girl put the beers in front of the men then sat down in the empty chair. "Not now, Marie," said Griffin. "This is too good." The woman gave him a disappointed look and got up to move on to another table. "Let me get this straight. Was the woman in the meeting with you and Will? Why do you need to talk to cows?"

Matt took a drink of beer and grunted as he slammed the glass down on the table. "Pay attention Griff. Why would the woman be in a meeting with me and Will? She was coming in the door and I ran into her and now she claims she is going lame and threw her hat at me." He placed the hat with blue ribbons on the table. "There it is, right there."

"Going lame?" Griffin began to laugh. "Why in the world is she going lame? I gotta tell you Matt, I think you're losing your touch.

I've had women throw a lot of things at me. Some nice, some not so nice, but a hat…"

"It's not funny," Matt interrupted with a scowl. She just threw it in my face and walked off. What kind of woman does that?"

Griffin picked up his beer and started to drink. "Was she pretty? Would I like her?"

"I guess she was. I just saw her for a moment." Matt began to think back to when the young woman looked at him in anger. "She was mad at the time and yelling that I had no sense. She had blue eyes. That's all I know…and blonde hair with a butterfly thing." He took another drink and slammed the glass down on the table again then motioned for Marie to bring them another round.

"She's got you riled up, whoever she is," said Griffin, intrigued by this woman who could make his ever so calm older brother babble on about a female this way.

"I'm not riled up. Finish your beer so we can go," Matt snapped. He was already irritated and now Griffin was beginning to annoy him. He regretted bringing it up.

"Well you could have fooled me." Griffin knew it was best to keep his mouth shut so the two sat there in silence and drank their beer. He smiled to himself, full of curiosity about the nameless girl with the blue eyes wandering the streets and the possibility that there was a woman who could best his brother.

CHAPTER 3

THE WIDOW'S RANCH

Will Spencer looked at Elizabeth with concern when she walked into his office. She appeared flustered and her clothes were in disarray He offered her a seat then sat down across the desk. He was a handsome man in his late forties with gray hair and a calm demeanor that set Elizabeth immediately at ease. He was known as an intelligent man with good business sense. One who acted with integrity and she hoped he would become a trusted ally.

"How was your trip?" he asked, feeling he already knew the answer. "You've had quite a journey."

"It was long, I'm afraid," said Elizabeth. "Please forgive me if I appear a bit frazzled. I had a run-in with a cowboy outside." She played with her hair, regretting that she threw away the hat which might have hidden the tangled mess it had become.

"A cowboy?" Will said. "I hope it wasn't one of our local men. Were you harmed? We'll contact the sheriff immediately. He will not tolerate harassment of women in any form."

"Oh no, nothing like that. Just a few unpleasant words, but all is well now," Elizabeth replied. She saw the concern on Will's face and thought it best to change the subject. "I'm looking forward to seeing the ranch."

"We're excited to show you. Margaret has worked for weeks to make sure everything is in order. We do have some things to go over first." He shuffled through a stack of papers on his desk. "There's the deed for you to sign and I took the liberty of asking Mr. Ferguson, the bank president, to set up your account. Of course, you may withdraw money anytime." As her accountant, Will was hired by her uncle to keep track of her expenses. He flashed his effervescent smile and handed her the documents for approval.

Elizabeth smiled courteously but was annoyed as she looked over the papers. Will didn't seem to have much faith in her abilities, which hurt her feelings. She would need to prove that moving west and buying a ranch was something she could do without failing.

"Margaret has planned a special meal for us. I guess I've already told you she has been a busy woman. I believe she's planning an afternoon tea with some of the ladies and probably a couple of other things she hasn't told me about. The people of this town are a friendly group and they'll be anxious to get to know you."

"I appreciate all that you and your wife have done, Mr. Spencer, but I'm use to a quiet life. I'm sure my uncle told you I am a widow. I've come to learn all I can about ranching, so I doubt I'll have much time for parties."

"Call me Will. We don't stand on ceremony around here. Margaret and I are hoping we'll all be friends. Of course, we respect your wishes but if I know my wife, you'll be dancing at the church social before the month is over."

Elizabeth smiled as she listened to him talk. He certainly seemed determined to see that she was accepted into the community and considering all they had done, she didn't want to hurt their feelings, but garden parties and an afternoon tea were not activities of interest.

She thought of Alex and cringed. What would he think about her sitting in a drawing room with a group of pretentious women holding her tea cup in a white-gloved hand? Dancing at a church social was out of the question. With whom would she dance? She needed to devote her energies to other things and would, at some point, politely need to make that clear to the Spencers.

"Well if you don't have any questions then we'll be off," said Will as he turned to get his jacket and ushered Elizabeth out the door to where his buggy stood waiting. She climbed to her seat and looked around as Will gave the reins a shake.

"This is a growing town," he began. "People poured in after the discovery of the Comstock Lode but it's supported by cattle and timber now. It does get wild on Saturday nights when the cowboys hit the saloons, but Sheriff Cameron does a fine job keeping the law."

Elizabeth took in the town as Will went on about the history of the area and the businesses along the street. It wasn't a bad town. There were a few buildings that could use some paint but there were also several large general stores, the hotel, millinery, two dress shops and a seed and supply. The church was larger than she expected to find.

"Margaret and I eat at the hotel restaurant every Sunday after church. Wonderful place. We hope you'll join us," he continued as the buggy stopped in front of a stately home surrounded by a wrought iron fence.

"There she is," he said, helping Elizabeth down. They started for the door where a woman stood waiting to greet them. She was an attractive woman who looked to be several years younger than Will. Taller than most women and perhaps a little too thin, in Elisabeth's opinion, her gracious smile was inviting, and Elizabeth was immediately drawn into the congenial environment of the Spencer home.

"You're here," she exclaimed and gave Elizabeth a big hug. "What a pretty girl you are. Let's sit for a moment and you can tell me about your day." She took her arm and led the way into a beautifully decorated parlor. Margaret offered a seat and cup of tea from the gold trimmed china pot arranged on the silver tray. Elizabeth gladly accepted and relaxed as she glanced around the room. Her old farm house was big with plenty of room, but the Spencer house was resplendent.

"I look atrocious," she said. "I can't tell you how much dust flies in the windows of a stage. I doubt I'll ever get it all off." She swept the skirt of her dress with her hand and nervously laughed. "I'm not much of a proper visitor."

"You look wonderful," said Margaret. "That stage can wear anyone out. It takes me at least a day to recuperate when I make a trip to San Francisco. I can't imagine what it must be like to travel on one from Salt Lake. Will doesn't like me to complain, but the passengers you meet are sometimes more dreadful than the ride. Would you care to freshen up before we eat? There's a room down the hall you can use."

"I'd like that," said Elizabeth and followed Margaret to a small wash room. Pouring water into a basin, she looked in the mirror and made a face when she saw the true condition of her appearance. "Oh my," she thought, what these people must think of me." There was a smudge of dirt on her cheek and strands of hair sticking out in all directions making her look like she was not in possession of her full senses. The young man outside Will's office came to mind. No wonder he called her ugly. Elizabeth made another face in the mirror then scolded herself for caring about the opinion of some back-road cowboy. Why should he matter? She'll never see him again. He was kind of cute though. Tall and well built, and he had a nice smile. It was something she noticed as he talked to the station manager. His tan complexion and dark eyes reminded her of Alex. Had they met under different circumstances, she might have been attracted to him.

Elizabeth was disgusted at her thoughts about this man and vowed not to think of him again.

She ran a brush through her hair and pinned it up with the hair pins which had all but fallen out. They were a gift from Alex. Turning around to look in the full length mirror she saw the torn, dirty hem dragging on the ground. "Yes, Elizabeth," she said out loud to herself. "You certainly made a wonderful impression."

They ate in the dining room on a long walnut table set with more china, silver and linen napkins. She remarked to Margaret that the china resembled the pattern of her mother's which was boxed and shipped west after the sale of the farm.

It was a pleasant meal filled with stories from Margaret and Will about life in Nevada and the people in town. Margaret talked about the stores. She listed which ones to frequent and which ones to avoid. She told Elizabeth about the tea she planned and the church bazaar to be held soon. Elizabeth knew she would be expected to attend and smiled politely.

"Neighbors are important out here," Will began as Margaret finished listing the menu choices available at the hotel restaurant. "It can be a rough life and people depend on each other. Good neighbors are a blessing and you've got some good ones. You'll learn that if you live here long enough."

"Their ranch is adjacent to yours," Margaret added. They have a daughter about your age and I know you two will hit it off. I've known her since she was a child and she's already asked when you might be available for dinner."

"They sound nice. I've liked everyone I've met so far." Well maybe not everyone, she thought and quickly pushed the cowboy out of her thoughts. Hopefully there aren't many more like him.

Once lunch was over, they left for the ranch and Elizabeth marveled at the countryside. It was beautiful, and she felt at home before they reached the crest of the hill where she caught her first glimpse of the house and barn. It was everything she wanted. It was a good size with abundant pasture land. There was plenty of water and the soil was fertile enough for crops, or so she'd been told.

"Elizabeth, this is Henry your ranch foreman and Luke, his right-hand man," said Will as she climbed from the buggy. "Henry is one of the most knowledgeable ranchers in these parts and Luke has plenty of experience. You'll not find any better than these two."

Elizabeth didn't think they seemed happy to see her as she smiled politely. Luke was friendly enough, but Henry's stern face made her feel uncomfortable, almost as if he didn't want her there at all. He was in his fifties with a touch of red mixed in with his silver hair. Henry did not strike her as a patient man and she wondered if Will had filled him in on her past.

Luke took off his wide-brimmed hat and nodded at her in what Elizabeth took as a sign of respect. His bald head was sunburned, and she wondered why he hadn't kept the hat on more often. "Why don't we show you around," he said apprehensively as if he was hesitant to bring up the topic. He glanced at Henry for a reaction and upon receiving a look of approval, steered Elizabeth toward the barn, pointing out the improvements as they went. "We've put a fresh coat of paint on everything, so the place looks brand new. Henry even built a flower box for the front porch. We figured you might like that."

Elizabeth glanced at Henry who looked away, disinterested. He can't be all bad, she thought. He built a flower box. "That was thoughtful," she said, and Henry shook his head in acknowledgment.

"We cleared a spot for a vegetable garden and you could put more flowers over there in the back..." Luke went on almost talking to himself as the others drifted into their own conversations.

"I come from farming people and don't know much about ranching but want to learn. I thought it would be a good idea if you and

I met each morning for breakfast to talk about things," she said to Henry.

"'Things?" Henry looked at her, surprised. "What things?"

"Day-to-day operations and what's going on. I know you were hired to run the ranch and I do respect your experience, but I still need to be a part of those decisions. It is, after all, my ranch and it is the only way I can learn."

Henry gave her a doubtful look. "Luke and I have been ranching for longer than you've been alive and running a ranch isn't something you learn overnight."

"I don't expect to," Elizabeth replied, rather disappointed. He made her feel her ability to learn was nil. "This is my life now and I'm more resilient than you think. I won't give up easily."

"They're waiting for you at the house," Henry said ending the conversation as he pointed to Will and Margaret who were standing on the porch.

The house was bigger than Elizabeth expected and beautiful. Some of her favorite pieces of furniture had been sent earlier and Margaret used them to their best advantage when arranging the rooms. The parlor was warm and inviting, although less formal than the one in the Spencer home, which suited her. There was even a piano.

"I don't play," Elizabeth said as she ran her hand over the smooth, polished wood then pressed a key to hear the sound.

"We shall provide lessons," Margaret answered with a smile. "There's nothing more comforting than beautiful music played on the piano. I daresay it can be romantic too."

The kitchen was huge in comparison to what she was used to and had a water pump at the sink. She never had such luxuries. She found several large bedrooms on the second floor and a real bathroom, unusual for a house in the country.

"This is more than I could have imagined," she said as they gathered together. I'm a bit overwhelmed."

"Your uncle wanted you to be comfortable and I hope you're pleased," said Margaret obviously delighted with her results and the pleasure Elizabeth showed. "Please let me know if there is anything you need."

Elizabeth was exhausted and said goodbye to the Spencers, more determined than ever to make this work. Life in Nevada would be tough, and it would take time to earn the trust of Henry and Luke, but she would not go back to Missouri. There was nothing to go back to. She would need to show a willingness to dig in and work as hard as the others.

After a hot bath she went to bed early and lying there, her head filled with a hundred thoughts about the past and what led her here. Now she was living in a town where she knew no one, on a ranch she didn't know how to run, trusting people she never met, but she was strong and bent on making this work, no matter what lay ahead.

CHAPTER 4

THE COWBOY, THE SNAKE AND THE SHOES

Elizabeth lifted her head off the pillow and sleepily looked around the room, confused for a moment as to where she was. The sunlight streamed through the thin sheers hanging from the window and she smiled. The first night in her new home was refreshing. It's amazing how a warm bath and comfortable bed can make such a difference.

She sat up and stretched, wondering what time it was. The house was quiet, something she was used to, and she was curious to see if Henry remembered they were to meet in the mornings. Throwing on a robe she headed downstairs and noticed the clock on the mantle said nine. She must have been more tired than she realized.

Elizabeth could see no one outside and assumed Henry and Luke had already started their work. What should I do on my first day, she wondered? There weren't many chores in the house. Margaret had seen to that. She arrived so late yesterday there wasn't much time for a full tour of her ranch. That, she decided, would be first on her list.

She quickly dressed, then made her way to the barn with the idea of performing her own inspection of the new land she now owned.

"Good Morning," Elizabeth said cheerfully, strolling into the barn where she found Luke mucking out the stalls. "What a beautiful day." She felt full of energy and ready to take on the world or at least the ranch and wanted to see everything she could.

"Good morning, Miss Elizabeth. Did you sleep well last night?" Luke asked. He grinned broadly as he paused from his work. "We sure are happy you're here."

"Yes, I slept wonderfully, although long past when I should," she replied. "Henry didn't seem too pleased to see me yesterday when I arrived. Is he always that grouchy? I thought for a moment he might escort me off the place."

"He's a tough bird, but a good man," said Luke. "A little hard to get to know at first. He'll come around."

"Tough bird is not the term I was thinking of," said Elizabeth as she clomped through the barn looking in each stall. "I'd like to go for a ride this morning. Is there a horse you can saddle for me?"

Luke frowned as he followed her around. She was wearing a dress which, in his opinion, was not suitable for a lady riding a horse with no side-saddle. Most women around these parts wore riding pants or one of those split skirts. They looked a sight better than a woman riding straddle-legged in a dress over a horse.

"Miss Elizabeth, Henry is off this morning looking for a lost calf, but he'll be back for lunch. If there's some place you'd like to go, he can take you then." Luke watched as she admired a saddle sitting on a rack and bridle hanging from a hook on the end of a stall.

"Oh, I don't need to be anywhere. I want to go for a ride and look around." She found a blanket in the corner and inspected it.

"I don't think Henry would like it if I let you go off on your own the first day. This ranch is large and it's easy to get lost if you don't know where you're going. It could be dangerous riding by your-self," Luke cautioned, thinking about Henry's reaction to Elizabeth's request.

"I have been riding since I was old enough to sit on a horse and my sense of direction is very good," Elizabeth said. "I used to go riding by myself all the time back home. I'll be fine."

"Are you planning to go dressed like that?" Luke asked. "Ladies don't usually ride straddled on a horse, wearing a dress."

"Well this lady does. If you could just get a horse for me to ride I would appreciate it," Elizabeth said, getting perturbed. "I won't be long. I just want to look around and will be right back."

"But Henry won't ..."

"I don't care what Henry thinks," Elizabeth hissed. "I'm asking for a horse to ride around my ranch. I'll be home before he gets back." She glared at Luke waiting for his response.

He took a deep breath exhaling loudly, as he walked to a stall mumbling and began to saddle one of the horses. Minutes later Elizabeth headed out for her ride, dress hiked up and hair blowing in the wind as the horse picked up speed and galloped away.

She rode some distance before stopping at a stream to rest. Elizabeth smiled as she led the horse to the water. This peaceful area with its shade trees reminded her of the creek back home. The warm sun felt good and as the horse walked to the edge to drink, she had the urge to wade in the cool water. She took off her shoes, pulled her dress up to her thighs and tucked it into the belt around her waist.

She waded in and giggled as her toes squished in the mud. Splashing around in the creek, Elizabeth was almost skipping through the water. She threw her arms out, turning in circles and flung her head back to gaze at the white puffy clouds in the sky.

"Is that how they teach you to dance where you come from?"

Elizabeth stopped suddenly and looked toward the bank to see a man leaning against a tree. She blushed as she glanced down at her bare legs sticking out of the water then glared indignantly at the cowboy. The same dusty cowboy she encountered outside Will Spencer's office. Why was he here? Did he have nothing better to do than to bother her?

"Sir, I'll thank you to leave this instant," Elizabeth said as she trudged through the water back to shore. "How dare you stand there gawking? You should at least have the decency to turn around while I get out." She reached the bank and pulled the skirt of her dress from the belt and it fell to the ground.

Matt Kelly pushed his hat back on his head with one finger, resisting the urge to smile at the sight of Elizabeth standing by the water with her toes dug into the mud. "Hmm, about that," he began. "See, you're trespassing on private property, so I figure I've got a right to gawk as much as I want."

"I don't see any signs posted saying I can't be here," snapped Elizabeth. "In fact, I believe you are the one trespassing so again, I will ask you to leave."

"This land is part of the Emerald ranch and the owners don't take kindly to people passing through," Matt said as he eyed her from head to toe. He had to admit she was attractive. Slim, delicate features, golden hair hanging down to the middle of her back, freckles on her nose and blue eyes. How could he forget those clear blue eyes which, as usual, were glaring at him like a bobcat ready to pounce?

"What are you doing out here by yourself?" he asked. "There are all kinds of men in these parts and some wouldn't hesitate to take advantage of a pretty girl wading in a stream with her dress hiked up to her..."

"Look cowboy, you tell Mr. Emerald I'm sorry for being on his property. It was a simple mistake." Elizabeth hated to apologize to this man who seemed to show up at the most inopportune time. "As for you, I'll thank you to keep your comments to yourself."

She watched with horror as Matt pulled a gun from his holster and pointed it in her direction. Would he really shoot her for mistakenly being on land belonging to someone else? "Please sir, I beg you."

Elizabeth screamed as Matt took aim and fired one shot, hitting a large snake lying on the ground within feet from where she was standing. She stared down at the headless body coiled on the bank and screamed again as she ran to the cowboy and wrapped her arms around his neck.

"Rattler," he said as he embraced her. "Could have killed you."

She held tight to him and he could feel the rhythmic pounding of her heart against his chest. He liked it and tightened his arms around her, smiling as he thought about the way she looked standing in the stream turning circles with her dress tucked in her belt. He liked that too.

She pulled away and glanced back at the dead snake, then turned back to Matt and hit him in the chest with both fists. "The rattlesnake could have killed me?" she shouted. "You could have killed me. I'm lucky I didn't drop dead from heart failure when you pulled out that gun. You should have warned me."

"I wasn't pointing at you," Matt said, amazed that this woman would now chastise him for saving her life. "What's wrong with you? You come riding out here by yourself, which was a foolish thing to do, traipsing around in the water like a school girl, and then almost get yourself killed by a deadly snake. Lady, I don't know where you come from, but you best be setting your sails for home because you won't last a day the way you're acting."

He picked Elizabeth up by the waist and lifted her to the saddle of her horse. Handing her the reins, he slapped the animal's hind quarter sending it galloping through the tall grass and stood baffled as he watched her disappear.

Elizabeth held on tight as the horse began to run. She was crying out loud, barely able to see from the flood of tears. She hated him. He had the audacity to watch her and not turn away while she lowered her skirt, as if she were a common saloon girl. Why shouldn't she be scared when he pointed the gun? He's a reckless cowboy and might just as easily have killed her as the snake. No one asked him to show up and save her life.

Elizabeth slowed the horse down to a walk, looking around for the way home. But he did save her life, she thought, and she didn't even thank him. She'd been ungrateful for his kindness and it was wrong. Oh, how she hated to be wrong and now she might never have a chance to tell him. Tell him what, she asked herself? That despite his constant annoyance every time they met, she was happy to see him and for a moment while she clung to him, she felt safer than she had since Alex was alive. "That's silly," she said out loud. "No man could ever make me feel that way again."

Henry struck the log with a forceful blow as the axe came down hard, splitting the wood in two. What had gotten into that girl's head going off by herself? Wild animals, criminals, Indians, any number of things could get her killed. Hell, they didn't have the first notion of where to start looking if she didn't make it back. How was he going to explain this to Will Spencer? He'd been out cutting wood for an hour since returning home and heard how Luke saddled a horse for her. Luke was a good man. They've worked together for many years. He had a big heart and found it difficult to say no to anyone, especially a young woman like Elizabeth. Henry blamed himself, though. He should have met with her for breakfast like she asked, then he could have stopped her from riding off.

"Miss Elizabeth is back," Luke shouted and they both turned and headed toward the house to meet her.

"Young lady, I ought to tan your hide," Henry said. Hearing his gruff voice made Elizabeth cringe. "What in the hell were you thinking?"

She turned to face Henry with swollen eyes and suddenly threw her arms around him and burst into tears. He stood there speechless and peered over at Luke who shrugged his shoulders, looking as dismayed as he was.

"What's happened to you? Are you alright?" Henry asked, looking her over to see if she was hurt. "We've been worried sick."

"I'm fine," Elizabeth answered, wiping the tears from her cheeks. "I saw a snake and was frightened, that's all." She had no intention of relaying the entire experience with the cowboy. It would add to her embarrassment.

"Where are your shoes?" Henry asked, looking down at her feet caked with dried mud. "Don't tell me you went riding through this countryside in bare feet?"

Elizabeth looked at Henry and Luke, speechless as she struggled for an explanation. The cowboy had thrown her on the horse and sent her off in a flurry. She never realized her shoes were still sitting by the tree where she had taken them off.

"I must have left them by the stream, where I stopped," Elizabeth said. "It was just for a moment and then I saw the snake and I guess I just hopped on the horse and left."

Henry grunted as he gave Elizabeth a bewildered look. This girl might be the death of him, he thought. "Well if that's not the most foolish thing I've ever heard. Where was this stream? Luke can go back and look for them while you calm down. We can't have you walking around like that."

"No," Elizabeth said. She panicked at the thought of Luke running into the cowboy and hearing the entire story. Was there no end to this misery, she thought? "I have another pair. Those were old, and I was about to throw them away. There's really no need to go back. Anyway, I've completely forgotten where I stopped."

"That makes no sense to me," Henry said throwing up his hands. "I give up trying to understand. You might want to go inside and find yourself some more shoes before you cut those feet. Probably wouldn't hurt to throw a little soap and water on them too."

Elizabeth hung her head as she slowly walked to the house, lightly treading over the rough ground. She lied to Henry. Those were her best pair of shoes and now the only ones she had left were, indeed, her old pair that were hardly presentable. She'd have to get new ones in town and hoped Henry or Luke would see their way to take her. What a disastrous day this was.

Elizabeth sat in the kitchen with her feet soaking in a pan of warm water when Luke knocked gently at the door and entered. "I just wanted to make sure you were alright. Sounds like you had quite a scare with seeing that snake. It's best to just back away from them and get out of their way as quick as you can when you see 'em."

"I'm much better now," Elizabeth said with a faint smile. "I didn't mean to worry anyone. I'm sure Henry will want to send me packing."

He was cutting those logs with a fury waiting for you to show up," Luke chuckled. "He's sore about it but has no intention of running you off, Miss Elizabeth. It's just the opposite. He figures you're not going to stay long so no need to get attached if you decide to up and leave us."

"Why would I do that? This is my home now," said Elizabeth, grabbing a towel to dry her feet. "Why does everyone think I'm going to give up and go home? It's irritating and I don't want to hear another word about it. You can tell Henry I have no plans to leave, but he need not feel he has to form an attachment with me, just the same."

"It isn't that, Miss Elizabeth. It's just that we've seen it before. Plenty of settlers come west looking for a new start and it isn't long before they can't make it in this wild land. Their crops don't grow, or their cattle die. Sometimes it's disease or death of a family member that'll drive them off."

"I'm afraid I've already suffered through the death and disease part," Elizabeth replied softly. "It's what drove me here."

"Of course, there's the part about Henry's family. He's never gotten over that," Luke said with a solemn face. "He had a family back east. Wife and two daughters, one about your age. Brought them out here from Kansas to get away from the war. He didn't want anything to do with that fight. They staked a claim on some land and tried their luck at ranching. Beef was in demand back then and both sides were willing to pay high prices."

Luke took off his hat and held it in his hands, looking haggard as he told the story. He seemed weary and Elizabeth found herself wishing she had held her temper when she spoke to this gentle man in the barn earlier in the day.

"Henry took his cattle back to Kansas to sell and while he was gone his youngest daughter took sick and died. It broke his heart. His wife couldn't stand to look at him anymore. She blamed Henry for the little girl's death because he brought them west to live. His wife said none of it ever would have happened if they had stayed in Kansas."

"What happened to them," asked Elizabeth. The death of Alex was so difficult for her that she couldn't imagine what it would be like to lose a child. Her heart broke for Henry as she listened.

"Henry's wife took their other daughter and moved back to Kansas. It's been years since he's heard from them and even longer since he's seen them. It's a wonder the man hasn't driven himself crazy with grief by now."

Elizabeth wiped away the tears trickling down her cheeks. It's true what they say, she thought, about never really knowing a person until you've walked in their shoes. She never would have guessed a hard-crusted soul like Henry would carry such a burden. He had felt loss and pain, as she had, and once again, she regretted any unkind words she had spoken about him.

"I need to apologize to Henry for the way I've acted and to you also," Elizabeth said. "I've been a spoiled child and that's not the kind of person I am. I have such a strong desire to make this new life work and it seems like everyone is dead set against me. It's like you're all waiting for me to fail. I won't last a day, that's what the cowboy said."

"Which cowboy was that?" Luke asked, watching Elizabeth's expression as she realized the blunder.

"No one," she replied brushing off the comment. "Just an old cowboy I ran into yesterday when I arrived. "I'm afraid he wasn't very complimentary."

"Was this cowboy the snake in the grass who scared you so much today?" Luke said

Elizabeth's eyes widened as she looked at Luke with shock. "How did you know? I mean...no...I really did see a snake."

Luke's skeptical face told Elizabeth he didn't believe her, so she told him about the cowboy who found her at the stream and that the shoes she left behind were not old ones, but ones purchased in St. Louis before she left. "I've made a mess of things, haven't I?"

"Nothing we can't fix," said Luke. "I'll just do as Henry suggested and go back to the stream to get them. It's no trouble for me."

"What if the cowboy is there?" said Elizabeth. "He might shoot you for being on the Emerald property. He pulled a gun on me, you know. Even though he was actually pointing at a rattler, but I don't think that's the point."

Luke laughed out loud. "Who was this cowboy? I know quite a few of the men who work for Tom and they all seem to have a good head on their shoulders. I can't imagine any of them wanting to run me off for retrieving a pair of forgotten shoes."

"I don't know his name," Elizabeth shrugged. "But he's rude and seems to show up where ever I go. He is an excellent shot, so you should keep that in mind if you run into him."

"Well, Miss Elizabeth, let's you and me make a deal," said Luke with a smile. "I'll hunt down your shoes if you don't mention our conversation to Henry. He doesn't like people getting in his business and I'm afraid he wouldn't appreciate me telling his story."

"And you promise not to tell him about the cowboy by the stream?"

"Not a word," Luke said as he stood to leave. "It's just between us friends."

"Yes," Elizabeth said as she gave him a hug. "Just between us friends."

CHAPTER 5

FINDING THE MYSTERY WOMAN

Matt slammed the front door and tossed his hat on a table. He walked across the room and plopped down in a chair next to the fireplace, put his feet up on a foot rest and looked at the pair of shoes he held in his hand. Running his fingers over the new leather he wondered where the woman ended up. He felt guilty for sending her off in anger. She was the most exasperating female he ever met and couldn't get her out of his mind. He was mad at her for reacting the way she did. If he hadn't spotted her horse and seen her in the water, she might not be alive now. She could be lying injured with no one to help. He was mad at himself for losing his temper. It was frustrating to find her shoes by a tree with no idea how to return them.

Griffin walked into the room biting into an apple. "Where have you been all morning?" he said as he wiped the juice off his chin. "Pa is spitting nails because that wagon wheel isn't fixed. He's been asking for you."

"I got tied up," Matt replied, still staring at the shoes. "I'll get to it tomorrow."

"You better get to it today or he'll make your life miserable. I'm not missing that card game at the Elkhorn tonight because Pa is on the warpath over you not getting your chores done."

"I'm not a kid, Griff," Matt snapped. "I don't need you to remind me about my work and I don't need Pa to tell me when to come and go." He leaned his head back in the chair and closed his eyes. His head was pounding, and his brother wasn't helping.

"Well, look who's acting like a bear with a sore head," Griff said. "What's been eating you the last couple of days? I can't say anything around you without getting my head torn off." He sat down next to Matt and picked up the shoes, looking them over with curiosity. "I'd love to know the story behind these."

Matt groaned when he opened his eyes and saw Griffin's mischievous wink as he held up the shoes. "Do these belong to your mysterious blue-eyed woman?" he said with a smirk.

"Unfortunately, they do," said Matt sighing heavily as he grabbed the shoes and closed his eyes again. "I have no idea what I've done to deserve that woman's wrath but every time I run in to her she takes a chunk out of my hide."

"First her hat and now these," Griffin said as he continued to goad his older brother. "I can't wait to see what you show up with next. I gotta tell you, I'm in awe of a man who can get a woman to give him her clothes every time they meet."

Matt opened his eyes once more and stared at Griffin then groaned before he filled him in on his morning. Griffin bit down on the apple as he listened and took note as Matt's facial expression changed from a pleasant smile when describing how cute Elizabeth was as he watched her dancing in the water to a dejected frown when he talked of her sudden anger and finally concern over sending this pretty blonde off on a galloping horse with her shoes still laying in the grass.

"You've got it bad, don't you?" said Griffin. "This whole thing that's going on between you and this girl. Why don't you ask around? Maybe she's staying with someone in town. It will be easy to spot a girl walking barefoot."

"There's nothing between me and this girl. In fact, she's infuriating. She hates me."

"Then why not throw the shoes away, or better yet, just leave them by the tree? Has it occurred to you that she might go back looking for them? Any chance you took them because it gives you an excuse to talk to her again?"

"Why would I want to talk to her again?" said Matt. "I just want to make sure she gets them back."

"Then you'll have to ask around until you find her." Griffin chuckled as he picked up the black shoes again and clicked the heels together. You might want to put these with that hat you saved until you track her down."

She'll probably throw them at me," Matt grumbled. "I better learn how to duck."

"That's my man," Griffin said as he slapped his brother on the back. "Now fix that wagon wheel so we can get out of here and have some fun."

CHAPTER 6

QUEEN OF HEARTS

The Elkhorn Saloon wasn't crowded when Matt and Griffin arrived, so they sat at a table farthest from the piano where there would be less noise. Matt waved when he caught the eye of Dutch Jordan and another gentleman as they walked in and motioned them over.

Dutch moved to town a couple of years ago, quickly becoming a regular in the Elkhorn. He was not much older than Matt but had a hardened look as if his life had not been easy. He kept to himself, so no one knew much about him. Dutch owned a few horses on a small piece of rented property, selling one occasionally to get by. He ran into Griffin the day before and explaining a business acquaintance was in town, asked if Griff and his brother, Matt, might be interested in a card game.

"Have a seat gentleman," Matt said. "We just got here." He pulled a deck of cards out of his pocket, laying them on the table. "Why don't you introduce your friend?"

"Jack Devlin," Dutch said, looking in the gambler's direction. "Like I was telling Griff, Jack is in town for a few days and I told him you two enjoy sitting down to a good game. He wanted to try his luck."

"I'm glad you looked us up, Dutch," said Griffin. "We always enjoy a little poker." He placed a wad of money in front of him. "Where are you from, Devlin?"

"Louisiana originally, but that was many years ago. I live in San Francisco now, although still enjoy traveling."

Jack studied Matt and Griffin as he sat down. He liked to get a gut feeling for the other players before the game started. He knew the Kelly brothers were fair players but would be no match for him. These two young men came ready to play. He glanced at the pile of money and knew if both men brought similar amounts, then he was set to make a bundle. He recognized Matt as the cowboy from the stage depot who pushed Elizabeth and a little payback for her inconvenience would be satisfying.

Jack was born in New Orleans, the son of a wealthy merchant. He was well-educated, having been groomed for a future in the family business, but defied those plans when he began a career as a gambler. Jack perfected his trade when he graduated to riverboats, then moved west where he eventually bought into a gambling house in San Francisco. That itch for travel never left him and he found himself looking for big stake games in other cities. Dutch offered to set the game up with the Kelly brothers as a favor to Devlin, so Jack decided to stay in town for another day.

Matt was curious about this stranger and his connection to Dutch. He found the man interesting, with his southern manners and refined speech. He was too refined, in his opinion, for a business associate. "What brings you to town, Mr. Devlin?"

"A horse," Jack said, settling back in his chair and lighting a cigar. "A perfect specimen. I've not seen one like him in quite a while and Mr. Jordan was able to acquire him on my behalf. I'm in town to pick him up."

"He must be some animal to come all this way," said Griffin. "Matt is a good judge of horses. He's been raising them since we were kids. He'd probably like to take a look, wouldn't you Matt?"

"Well, like most men, I always like to admire a fine animal," Matt said, leaning back in his own chair and casually picking up the cards, shuffling them in his hands. He'd seen this gambler before but was having trouble placing him. "You plan to race him?"

"As a matter of fact, I do," replied Jack, puffing his cigar and looking around for one of the working girls. "I've searched for a thoroughbred with a strong bloodline for years. This stallion is imported from England. He comes from champion stock and I'll have him paying for himself in no time."

"It can't all be about money, Mr. Devlin," said Matt. "A horse as valuable as your thoroughbred should be loved like a woman...treated like a precious jewel."

"Don't worry, Mr. Kelly," Jack said with a hint of disdain as he blew a ring of smoke into the air. "I know how to treat a horse...and a woman. Not all men possess that knowledge. Some never see that precious jewel, even when she's standing in front of him, waiting to be held and cherished."

"How about a drink? All this talk is making me thirsty," Griff called out. "Marie, can you bring us a bottle?"

"And a new deck of cards," added Jack, never taking his eyes off Matt.

"And a new deck of cards from behind the bar," Griffin nervously repeated. "What do you say we get started? I feel lucky tonight."

Matt threw in his ante then slowly shuffled the deck moving it toward Griffin who cut the cards as the others watched. He dealt five cards to each man, and then placed the deck on the table as he looked at his own hand. The others did the same and starting with Dutch, called out the number of new cards they wanted, discarding the unwanted ones.

Jack stared at his hand. He was holding three tens. He looked at Griffin who brushed his lips with his index finger as he sat in deep thought. Dutch had the face of a man who knew he was beaten but Matt sat stone-faced with his cards folded in his hands as if he had no interest in the game at all. Devlin smiled to himself as he looked at the young man with the indifferent expression, sitting across from him. The younger brother would be easy to read but Matt would be a challenge and that was something Jack enjoyed.

"I can't believe I'm gonna have to fold right out of the chute," said Dutch as he threw down his cards in disgust.

Jack chewed on the end of his cigar as he glanced at each player once more. He watched Griffin rub his bottom lip with a finger. He has something he can play, thought Jack. Not aces. Griff isn't acting like a man holding aces, but he's definitely got something. He hadn't figured Matt out yet. It would take more than one hand for that. He picked up a bill from his pile of cash and pitched it on the table.

Griffin sat motionless for a moment before throwing in his money and calling. He took a drink and exhaled loudly as he tensely looked to his bother.

Matt knew his hand wasn't good enough. A pair of eights doesn't beat much. Devlin had thrown money on the table, meaning he had cards worth betting on. The gambler is too good to bluff this early in the evening. Griffin was fidgety, and Matt suspected his brother might have a winning hand so knew better than to bet against him. He placed his cards on the table. "I'm out," he said.

Griffin pulled a pair of jacks from his hand and smugly slapped them down. He took another drink and glanced at Matt while waiting for Devlin to show his cards. Matt has always been the better player and Griff enjoyed times when he was the one to come out on top.

Jack stared at the three tens. It would be easy to scoop up the money and move to the next hand but that wasn't what he wanted. He liked his opponents to feel comfortable. People tend to bet larger amounts when they're relaxed and winning a few hands was the best way to make a player confident. Matt had not given himself away so far. There was no squirming in his seat or nervous twitch. He paid little attention to the other players. He was guarded and would play too cautiously until Jack could ease the tension in the game. He would let the younger brother win this round. The evening was just getting started and there was plenty of money to make. He separated two of the tens from the rest of his cards and placed them face up on the table as he folded the rest in his hand and laid them on the discard pile, showing no emotion as Griffin breathed a sigh of relief and smiled.

"See, I told you I was feeling lucky tonight," Griff said as he nudged Matt.

Matt's eyes met Devlin's and for a moment he thought there was a glimmer of a smile. That was unusual for a man who just lost money. Even more unusual was the two tens he played. He couldn't imagine a gambler like Devlin setting his hopes on a simple pair of tens. He slapped his brother on the back and smiled. "Nice hand, Griff. You're going to need more of that luck because this next one is all mine."

The next hand did, indeed, belong to Matt while the third to Devlin. As the evening progressed, the men fell into a cadence, dealing and betting that included a touch of laughter. Jack puffed on his cigar and watched the Kelly brothers as they teased each other continually. He was from a large family but never felt the close sibling bond these two shared. Griffin would shout with delight when he won, then chide Matt over his card-playing skills. Matt was more reserved with his achievements but would not fail to remind his younger brother who the better player was as he raked money from the center of the table into a neat pile in front of him.

What Dutch Jordan lacked in card playing, he made up for in other ways. He became the keeper of the bottle, as he called himself, and divvied up the whiskey, although the others were smart enough to keep their wits about them while they played, leaving Dutch to down the lion's share. Marie and some of the other women hovered close to him in hopes of sharing the spoils of his winnings at the end of the evening, but Dutch was destined to go home empty-handed on all accounts.

Their table drew an audience after Dutch, attempting to boost his reputation as an important cog of Elkhorn Saloon society, made sure other patrons knew a gambler of Jack Devlin's ability was playing at their table. It became more like a parlor game as men sauntered over to watch, offering advice or bemoaning mistaken strategy while they reminisced about other big stakes games they'd seen. Onlookers cheered with the winner and grumbled with the losers as the winning hand was laid on the table. Once, after Griffin threw out three jacks to beat Matt's two aces, there was such a commotion the piano music stopped, and someone sent for the sheriff, thinking that a fight had broken out and gunfire was likely to follow. Jack Devlin restored order when he offered to buy a round for the house and the music began again, but not before Sheriff Cameron strolled in and made his presence known.

"You four behaving yourselves? I've had a complaint," Cameron said as he surveyed the table decorated with stacks of money and half-filled whiskey glasses. He was a tall, muscular man in his early twenties with a quiet demeanor. He shot an inquisitive look at Devlin as the gambler sat quietly shuffling the cards. "I know these three, but I don't believe I recognize you."

"This is Jack Devlin, sheriff," said Dutch. "He came in on the stage yesterday afternoon. He's here to buy one of my horses." Jordan looked nervously at Matt for help with an explanation for their gathering.

"We all got a little carried away, Reece," explained Matt, somewhat embarrassed at the presumed scolding by the sheriff. "You know anytime Griff wins a hand there's bound to be a celebration, seeing how that only happens about once a year."

Griffin's mouth fell open as he raised his finger in protest when the sheriff spoke. "Well I wish I woulda been here for that. You're never gonna hear the end of it, Matt."

He watched Jack swirl the whiskey around in his glass, trying to remember if he had seen his face on a wanted poster or heard his name in connection with a crime. "Looks like you've had a pretty successful night. Do you play a lot of poker, Mr. Devlin?"

"From time to time," answered Jack as he lit another cigar. I've had excellent company this evening and commend these gentlemen on their expertise. We'd be happy to have you join us if you'd like. I'm sure Marie could find another chair and an empty glass."

"Thanks for the offer, but I don't make it a habit of playing when I'm on duty. I believe I'll sit for a time and watch." The sheriff looked at Griffin and smiled. "It gives me a chance to keep my eye on these Kelly brothers. Maybe I can witness Griff perform a miracle by winning another hand."

Griffin grinned and shook his head. "I don't believe our sheriff has recovered from the last time he encountered me in a game of cards, Mr. Devlin. His money clip has been a little lighter ever since."

"I guess we forgot to mention we've known Reece since we were kids," said Matt as he watched Sheriff Cameron pull up a chair. "It's usually been my job to keep him out of trouble and not the other way around." Matt moved his finger between Reece and Griffin, pointing at both. "They're two peas in a pod."

"I'm delighted to meet you, sir," said Jack as he bowed his head in the sheriff's direction. "May I say you've made an excellent choice in friends? I've found both young men to be amiable competitors."

"That's nice, because I usually find them to be an ornery bunch," replied Reece. "You got anymore of those cigars?"

Jack smiled as he pulled another cigar from his suit jacket and handed it to the sheriff. He was disappointed Reece Cameron declined to play as he felt the sheriff was a cunning adversary. It was obvious he was a man of detail. His eyes constantly moved about the room taking note of activities around him. Jack was sure the sheriff had quickly counted the piles of cash when approaching the table earlier and was aware that he and Matt were the most successful players. Still, even though Devlin had done nothing wrong, in his line of work, he felt more comfortable interacting with the law at a distance. He hadn't won as much in the game as intended but it was time for him to leave.

"Did I understand you to say you came in on the afternoon stage yesterday, Mr. Devlin?" asked Matt. He'd been thinking of something Dutch Jordan said earlier and it suddenly occurred to him why Jack's face seemed familiar. He was at the stage depot when Matt picked up the saddle. Matt's face turned red as that image flashed in his mind. Devlin was there alright, standing next to the woman who has been the plague of his life for the past two days.

"That's correct," replied Devlin who noticed the changed coloring in Matt's face as he pensively stared in Jack's direction. "After spending some time in Denver, I caught the stage in Salt Lake and arrived late afternoon to meet Mr. Jordan."

Jack wondered if Matt finally caught on that Elizabeth Rogers was standing next to him when he slammed into her with the saddle. There was some satisfaction for Jack in knowing this young cowboy now found himself in the precarious position as combatant in an unspoken duel for the young lady's honor. It had been Jack's intention all evening to relieve Matt Kelly of as much of the cowboy's worldly wealth as possible to compensate for the discourteous treatment he had shown Elizabeth at the station, even if that cowboy hadn't been aware of his plan. Perhaps he had time for one more hand.

Matt sat motionless staring at Devlin, a wave of thoughts tumbling in his brain. What was the pretty blonde woman doing in the company of this gambler, he thought? Was she his ward or relative? His face drained of color as quickly as it had reddened, and his stomach began to twist in a knot when he thought of the possibility that she might be his wife. If so, why would he let her wander off alone on horseback without an escort? He resented Jack Devlin for his attachment to the young woman and would like nothing better than to send him packing.

"It's getting late, gentlemen and I have many things to do before I leave tomorrow," said Jack. "I propose one more hand before we say goodnight. One that, I guarantee, will not be for the faint of heart." He picked up the bottle of whiskey and refilled the glasses as he looked at Matt with renewed animosity.

Dutch emptied his glass then sleepily laid his head on the table. "I think I'm gonna have to pass on this. I'm out of whiskey and out of money. It's time for me to say goodnight."

"What do you have in mind?" laughed Griffin. "Just throw all our money on the table and take a card?"

"Something like that," answered Jack, stroking his thin mustache. "I propose we count our winnings now, with the high man capturing the privilege of setting the ante for the hand. I believe you'll find that I will be that man."

Griffin picked up his cash and looked at Matt whose sympathetic expression told his brother he agreed that Devlin had probably won the most money for the evening. Griffin began to count as Devlin continued to explain.

"There will be no further betting once the ante is set. We will play five-card draw as usual with the best hand winning."

"So, you want us to bet on a hand we haven't seen?" asked Matt. He was intrigued and assumed this was Devlin's way of cleaning them all out before leaving town. He's a confident man, thought Matt, knowing his own winnings had all but matched Devlin's for the evening. He grumbled to himself in disgust at the gambler's arrogance, then picked up his money and began to count.

"I propose to set the ante at one thousand dollars," Jack said when the money was tallied. "If you can't match that amount you are, of course, allowed to ask another for monetary help or in lieu of cash, may make up the difference with other valuables such as your horse or saddle or pistol." He placed his money in the center of the table and folded his hands on his chest as he waited for Matt and Griffin to respond.

Griff looked relieved as he counted his stash once more, followed by the announcement that he was significantly short of the set amount. "I've had Rascal since I was young and I'm not taking the chance of losing him in something like this when I don't even know what cards I'll be holding. I guess I'm going to have to call it a night, the same as Dutch." He leaned back in his chair and looked at the sheriff who shook his head derisively.

Matt didn't like the idea of the game at all. It was not a matter of money. He had more than enough cash to cover the ante. He was not a risk taker, especially when it came to finances, but his sudden dislike for Devlin, once he connected him with the nameless blue-eyed girl, egged him on. He was jealous of this man and although it went against all reasoning, Matt wanted this chance to beat Jack Devlin in the last hand, but he wanted his own terms.

"I don't care to match your ante," Matt said. "Instead I propose another bet. Five hundred dollars and my horse against your matching money and horse." All noise in the roomed seemed to stop except for the tinkling of piano keys in the background and a sudden snort from a sleeping Dutch Jordan. Griffin and the sheriff glanced at each other, nodding with approval.

"That's preposterous," said Jack, losing his calm composure. "My beautiful animal against a trail beaten work horse. How could you possibly think I would accept such an idea? If you want an equal bet, then I'm sure Mr. Jordan can provide a comparable animal for this purpose."

Jordan snorted again on cue and raised his head when he heard his name, looked around the room, then lowered it again and dozed off.

"I don't think Dutch is in a condition to provide much of anything tonight," Griffin snickered. "Besides, we've seen his stock and he's got nothing to compare to any of Matt's animals. You'll be getting your money's worth with this horse." He smiled broadly as he looked at Matt only to see his brother's disapproving glare. "Not that Matt is going to lose. I mean, you both have the same chance."

"I can attest to the value of Matt's horse, Devlin," added the sheriff. "He's known in the county as a fine animal. I guarantee the owner of the Emerald would stand by that animal if things came to it."

Jack cursed himself for getting into this situation. He had to give credit to this cowboy for the way he maneuvered into this bargaining position. He was smarter than Jack had given him credit for, but Jack would not be outdone.

"Well, young Mr. Kelly, it seems you and your horse come well recommended by the law. Certainly, if the owner of a ranch as large as the Emerald would certify your horse then I would find it difficult to argue. I will, however, insist the bet shall be seven hundred dollars plus the horse and I will hold Sheriff Cameron to his guarantee that your animal is of the highest quality."

"Seven hundred it is, and I trust that your thoroughbred is everything you've presented him to be," said Matt as he counted out his money and threw it in the center of the table. "I believe it's your deal Mr. Devlin, unless you would like a third party to act as dealer for this hand."

Dutch Jordan was carried to another table in the corner of the bar and one of the bartenders sat down in his spot. He opened a new deck and shuffled as the patrons once again gathered around to watch. Griffin and Sheriff Cameron moved back and left the table to the two players and the bartender who repeated the wager out loud to each player, waiting for their acknowledgment before counting out five cards to each.

Matt slowly separated his cards and looked at his hand. His heart sank deep in his chest and that familiar churning returned to his stomach. Four, five, six, eight and a queen. He thought of the young woman standing by the creek in the mud and found it ironic that his queen was a heart. He might as well be the joker because this hand was lost as far as he was concerned. He couldn't imagine Devlin with anything worse than one queen and an incomplete straight. He berated himself for taking on such a foolish bet all because of jealousy over a female with dirty feet. He looked at Devlin who showed no signs of emotion which was not surprising. Matt had a strong desire to down the whiskey in his glass to gather one last ounce of courage but thought Devlin might take it as a sign of weakness or at the very least a bad hand. He jumped slightly as Dutch Jordan snorted and rolled over in the corner. Dutch and Griffin were the smartest players of the evening. At least they would get a good night's sleep.

He needed a seven for a straight, so he said goodbye to his queen of hearts as he pulled her from his hand, slid the card face down toward the bartender, and pulled back a replacement.

Jack also fought the urge to empty his glass, but in celebration and not despair. He was holding three aces and felt confident he would be leaving for Sacramento a happy man. The evening had been a success. He studied Matt's face but there was no sign of emotion. Matt only threw away one card, so he must have two pair. That was easy enough to figure out. He sat for a moment watching the deadpan stare of the cowboy, wondering if he was confident in his hand or if he might be in agony over the thought of losing. He'd been in Matt's shoes many times and would be there again many more before his gambling days were finished. He enjoyed these anxious moments before all cards were revealed. It was akin to having a wild animal in your sights and that exhilaration you feel seconds before you pull the trigger. Once the gun is fired, the thrill of the hunt is gone. He discarded and picked up two new cards. A ten and jack. They were no help to him.

The piano music stopped, and the pianist walked toward the table where the three men sat. It was late and only a handful was left to witness the game. Griffin and the sheriff kept them closely corralled on the sides of the table away from the players so no one saw their cards. The air was thick but not a person moved as the bartender motioned for the men to show their hand.

Jack laid his aces out one at a time amidst the awes from those watching. Dutch Jordan mumbled in the corner, but no one paid attention. Their eyes were on Matt as he sat dry-mouthed with stomach knotted, studying the five cards he held in his hand. His queen of hearts had come through for him and exchanged her place in line with the lucky seven he needed. He fanned his cards and laid the straight on the table atop a pile of money and breathed a sigh of relief.

The crowd was silent as they stared at the four, five, six, seven and eight spread out in ascending order until Griff threw his hat in the air and let out a shout that was heard in the hotel lobby down the street. This was followed by a jubilation of noise and clapping that, some would later claim, shook the very foundation of the Elkhorn Saloon as the bartender announced Matt Kelly the winner and owner of Jack Devlin's prize, pure-blooded, thoroughbred and seven hundred dollars in cash.

CHAPTER 7

JACK AND A QUEEN

Reece Cameron ran the tin cup back and forth against the iron bars of the cell door making a clanking sound that reverberated throughout the room. Matt groaned and pulled the pillow over his head. Griffin was lying on his stomach with one arm hanging over the side of the wooden framed cot, still asleep, unaware of the continual clatter.

"You're going to have to find somewhere else to sleep," said Reece, throwing the door open and prodding his friends. "Hotel Jail Cell is now closed. I know it was easier for you three to sleep here last night but I may need these beds for actual criminals. Besides, Devlin agreed to meet you at the hotel to officially turn over ownership of that horse."

Matt threw the pillow on the floor, squinting at the sheriff. It was late when the celebration ended at the Elkhorn. Everyone in town, who was still awake at that hour, drifted in as news of the card game spread. Every miniscule detail of the evening was repeated for all who entered and every man who heard, felt duty bound to buy a congratulatory drink for the winner, while Jack Devlin sat silently in his chair, sipping his scotch and smoking his tiny cigar.

"What time is it?" Matt asked. "We need to be there at ten." He sat up slowly and watched Reece pulling Griffin out of bed by his legs. "You might want to tie him to a mule and drag him out."

"I'm up," mumbled Griff and he shook his legs until the sheriff let go, and then rolled over. "Does this hotel have any coffee?"

"There's a pot in the other room," answered Reece. "It's already nine and if you two hurry we still have time for breakfast. I rode out this morning and told your pa you decided to spend the night in town. I didn't want him worrying about you two."

"Did you tell him about the game?" asked Matt

"No, I thought I'd let you do that. He was grumbling about some dinner party he's having tonight for the Spencers and a widow that moved into the old Butcher place. He wants you home early. He's got a list of chores for you."

"I thought Henry Turner bought the Butcher ranch," said Griffin. "He's been living there for months."

"Henry is just running the ranch. It's owned by a widow from back east. Will Spencer was telling your pa that the widow lives there now, and he thinks it would be a good idea for everyone to meet. He wants to make a good impression so he's having her and the Spencers for dinner."

Reece snickered as he walked to another cell where Dutch Jordan was stretched out. "The sight of you two ought to give her a fine idea of what to expect from her new neighbors." He kicked at Jordan's bed and shook his shoulder. "Dutch, time to get up. We got things to do."

Matt stuck his hand in his pocket as he headed out the door, making sure the seven hundred dollars was still safely tucked away. He pulled out a playing card and smiled. During the mayhem following the game, he searched through the discard pile looking for his queen of hearts. She was his lucky charm, a guardian angel that saw him through his great battle and he wanted to keep her close.

"What in the world is an old widow going to do with a cattle ranch?" Griffin grunted as he poured the coffee.

"She's probably got more money than sense, or maybe she's running from the law," replied Matt with a smile. "We may need to have Reece investigate."

"Yeah, she may decide Pa is a pretty good catch once she sees the ranch."

"Pa may decide she's a good catch," Matt chuckled. "Heck, we could have ourselves a new step-mother by Christmas."

"We'll have Reece hold our room here at Hotel Jail Cell," teased Griffin. "Just in case we're left out in the cold."

Once Dutch was awake the four men walked to the hotel. The men decided before they left the Elkhorn that Devlin would meet them there. The sheriff asked Dutch to identify the animal as the race horse he had sold to Devlin. Sheriff Cameron went along to make sure no one had second thoughts regarding the wager made and that things went smoothly.

Devlin was waiting for them when they arrived. Nothing could be done at this point, Jack thought. He brought it on himself. He spent the evening setting the cowboy up and preparing him for the kill. He bought the whiskey, let Matt win enough hands to keep up interest and humored the antics between the two brothers. Jack knew it was not Matt Kelly's fault he lost the card game and his thoroughbred, but as he sat across the table from him now, his loathing for the man grew with every passing moment.

He had no intention of leaving town. That horse was important to his future and he wasn't ready to let him go that easily. He was hoping Matt would give him a chance to win his thoroughbred back, so he decided to bide his time for a few more days. He needed to fix this situation.

It was a short walk to the livery stable. Dutch verified the horse and Jack courteously shook Matt's hand signifying the conclusion of the transaction, then walked out leaving the others behind chattering with excitement. He headed back to the hotel in hopes of catching up on lost sleep from the night before and passed Miller Mercantile.

Miller's was one of the largest general stores in town and popular, thought Jack. Ladies were streaming in and out of the door from all sides, leaving little room for him on the sidewalk. Out of curiosity, he paused for a moment and peered in the door, smiling with satisfaction when he spotted a pretty blonde woman looking at shoes. Perhaps the day wouldn't turn out to be as bleak after all. He removed his hat and smoothed his dark hair, then straightened his tie before entering the store.

"Mrs. Rogers, what a pleasant surprise. How is ranch life suiting you?" He smiled and offered a slight bow as he tipped his hat.

"Mr. Devlin," Elizabeth said. Her eyes lit up at the sight of her friend from the stage. "Ranch life has been a bit of an adjustment. I'm afraid I'm already in need of a new pair of shoes. And what of you? I thought you'd be in Sacramento now with your new horse."

"I've been detained on business, so my travels west will have to wait, but seeing you has made my extended stay worth it. It will give me an opportunity to take a lovely young woman such as you to dinner this evening, if you would permit."

Elizabeth looked at the shoes she was holding and blushed. "Mr. Devlin..."

"Please, call me Jack."

"Well then, Jack, I'm honored you asked me but I'm afraid I have other plans," said Elizabeth, a bit nervous about getting an invitation from a gambler like Jack Devlin. Still, he has behaved like a gentleman toward her and she might consider his offer on any other day. "Perhaps another time if you're still in town."

"Would you at least allow me to escort you while you shop? I've been told I have a talent for carrying packages." Jack tipped his hat and bowed so deeply he smacked the back of a woman's leg with his hand as she passed by, causing her to shriek and hop a step before scurrying on to another part of the store.

Elizabeth reddened and giggled, hiding her face with the pair of shoes she was holding. She wondered who the woman was and if she might run into her again on another day. More importantly, would the woman remember this incident?

"Mr. Devlin," she whispered. "You may escort me while I shop but only if you promise to behave and not accost the other women."

"I give you my word," Jack said, turning around to see if the area was clear before bowing again. "Where to next Malady?"

"After I leave here then on to the seed and supply. Do your talents include carrying baling wire and a sack of garden seeds?

"I will relish the challenge, but you must allow me to take you to lunch to redeem myself for any embarrassment I may have caused," said Jack.

"I need to meet up with my ranch foreman, Henry. He drove me to town and is somewhat of a stern fellow. I'm afraid he would frown if I were late. I've already gotten on his bad side."

"Then by all means, purchase your wares and let us be off. I would not rest if I were the blame for your tardiness and the scorn of your ranch manager. You can tell me about your adventures as we walk."

Elizabeth picked out a pair of shoes along with a new dress she would need for special occasions. Margaret Spencer had made good on the promise to fill her social calendar with dinner invitations and social gatherings including one set for this evening, forcing Elizabeth to rethink her wardrobe. Her clothes were all too practical and not suited for what Margaret had planned. She wore her best dress the day she arrived, and it was still covered in dust with a torn hem and since Luke had never recovered her shoes at the creek, she was forced to buy a new pair. Jack's smile showed his approval of her selection, so she made her purchase and they were off to the seed and supply.

"The Spencers are friends of my uncle," Elizabeth began as she told Jack about the people she met since arriving. "And from St. Louis so it's almost like being home again, which can be a good thing and a bad one. She's very chic and their home is magnificent. She wants me to attend parties which is why I'm having dinner with them this evening at the Emerald ranch. Mr. Emerald is the biggest rancher in the state."

"Mr. Emerald?"

"Yes, the Emerald ranch borders my land and Will thinks it's important we all get along. Apparently, there is a daughter my age. Henry is all for it too."

"Tell me about your ranch, are you happy with it? I must say it seems to agree with you. Your face is radiant as you speak."

"It's everything I was hoping for," replied Elizabeth. "So beautiful. You should see the house. Margaret had everything ready when I arrived, but I do want to add my own touches and the first thing I need is a vegetable garden and some flowers. It's why we're stopping at the seed and supply. I have a long list..."

Elizabeth paused mid-sentence and stared at the street as they walked, craning her neck around bystanders and horses to get a look at a man sitting atop a beautiful buckskin horse. It's him, she thought, as a kaleidoscope of butterflies fluttered in her stomach. The cowboy waved to a group of men standing on the sidewalk as they called out his name.

"Elizabeth?" asked Jack.

"Yes?" she said turning her attention again to Devlin.

"I think I've lost you. I was asking when you were to meet your ranch manager and if he would be available to load your supplies?" He looked toward the street and saw Matt Kelly riding the thoroughbred and realized their conversation was interrupted by the cowboy. I see you recognize him from the stage depot." He was annoyed that Matt had not only won the horse but also the attentions of Elizabeth.

"Among other places. I've run into him a couple of times since the stage and must say his manners haven't improved. He's quite irritating and I have no use for him," she answered as she turned toward Matt again. He was looking in her direction and when their eyes met, she quickly turned away, embarrassed that he had seen her. Pretending she hadn't noticed, she took Jack's arm and quickened her step, looking straight ahead. "We need to hurry, I'm sure Henry is waiting."

But Matt had noticed and was slowly getting angry. There was the mysterious young woman walking with Devlin and his jealousy came back. She must have accompanied him on this trip. He signaled his horse to speed up and galloped down the street leaving Elizabeth to follow him with a nonchalant glance until he disappeared.

When Elizabeth reached the seed and supply, she found Henry sitting out front in the wagon with a disapproving stare as they approached. Once again, she felt uncomfortable and wondered what she had done wrong this time.

Henry was cold as she introduced him to Jack and Elizabeth didn't like the way he was acting. She had done nothing wrong. Jack Devlin was a friend and she had every right to walk with him. She was chilly toward Henry in return and less than friendly as she spoke.

"Jack has asked me to have lunch with him," she said, although she had lost her appetite and wanted nothing more than to go home.

Her day was once again ruined by seeing the cowboy and she was angry with herself for feeling that way.

"We need to get back. If you still want your supplies to plant that garden, then let's get inside and pick out what you need. You've been gone all morning," said Henry with his disapproving look. "You have plans for the evening and there are chores to be done."

"But Mr. Devlin has been kind enough to help carry my packages," Elizabeth answered with her own disapproving look. It was true she had changed her mind about Jack's invitation to lunch, but she didn't like Henry's attitude.

"I'm sure you appreciate his help," Henry said. "But I'm responsible for keeping your ranch running smoothly and I can't do my job if I'm waiting around for you all day."

Elizabeth looked at Jack with pleading eyes. She was embarrassed with the fuss Henry was causing. He was treating her like a child, but she had no desire to make a scene in front of him. "I suppose Henry is right. Would you mind if I beg off this time? I do have plans for later and it would be best if we call it a day."

Jack glared at Henry but kept his gracious manner with Elizabeth. He resented Henry's attitude toward him and butting into Elizabeth's business when it wasn't his place. He understood now why she found him abrasive.

"Whatever you think is best, Mrs. Rogers," he replied stiffly. "Perhaps another time." He excused himself and turned back toward the hotel, more determined than ever to encourage their friendship. He didn't like to lose and neither Matt Kelly nor Henry Turner would get in his way.

Elizabeth purchased the things she wanted at the seed and supply and climbed in the wagon without saying a word to Henry. She waited until they were almost back to the ranch before breaking her silence.

"Henry, I know Will has a lot of faith in your abilities as a ranch manager and I'm sure he's right in his opinion, but I object to the way you spoke to me in front of Jack Devlin. I am not a child and won't be treated like one. I've been on my own for some time now."

"You may have been on your own, but I doubt you've come across men like Jack Devlin," said Henry. "I've seen 'em before. Dressing in their fancy suits, traveling from town to town, grabbing people's money in their poker games and taking advantage of nice young ladies like you and I won't have it. I'm responsible for your ranch and that means I'm responsible for you."

"Jack Devlin has been nothing but kind to me since I met him," said Elizabeth. "I can take care of myself and I can have lunch with whomever I want, and I'll thank you to mind your own business."

Henry grunted and mumbled to himself. "I suppose you can, but I don't like it."

Elizabeth stared at the scenery as the wagon rolled along. Why was it that every time she started to feel comfortable in her new surroundings, something happened to make her feel lonely? If that cowboy wasn't ruining her day, then Henry was. She thought of what Luke had said about Henry losing his family. Maybe he's lonely too. Still, that's no excuse, she thought, as she stiffened her chin and sat indignantly. It was obvious they were both stubborn and would never agree on Jack Devlin or anything else for that matter but as Henry pointed out, Jack would be gone in a few days. There was no harm in enjoying his company while he was in town and if it means living with Henry's displeasure then so be it.

CHAPTER 8

EMERALD SURPRISE

The front door opened almost before Elizabeth reached the steps of the porch which wrapped around the country home like the white brim of a summer hat. A large man with graying hair walked out, smiling broadly as he slapped Will Spencer on the back.

"Good evening," he proclaimed so loudly he practically shouted. "Always good to see my old friends." He offered Elizabeth his arm as she reached the thresh hold, "Welcome to the Emerald, young lady. It's a pleasure to meet you. Come inside and meet the rest of the Kelly family."

Elizabeth glanced demurely around the room as she entered the parlor where the others were waiting. The light from the enormous fireplace gave the room an inviting glow and she met equally warm smiles from her hosts. In addition to the gentleman who was excitedly talking with Will about cattle and lumber, there was a beautiful girl about twenty who, Elizabeth thought, must be the daughter Margaret was so anxious for her to meet. She stood next to a young man several years older. Thank goodness I bought this new dress, she thought. I would have looked as drab as an old shoe around these people who, as far as Elizabeth could tell, weren't named Emerald after all.

"I'm a little confused," she blurted out suddenly. "I thought your last name was Emerald. I've heard so much about your ranch, I guess I just assumed..."

"No," the gentleman laughed. "Although I see how it could be an easy mistake. My name is Tom Kelly. My wife named our ranch the Emerald on account of our family being Irish and from the Emerald Isle. She passed several years ago."

"I'm sorry for your loss," said Elizabeth, embarrassed she brought it up. She stood fidgeting, afraid to say anything else.

"Kelly, being a shade of green much like emerald, was Mama's favorite color," the young lady said. "It all seemed to fit together for our family. I'm Rachel. Forgive us for the short notice. We only heard yesterday that you arrived. We appreciate your kindness in taking time to have dinner with us. I know how busy you must be. There's always so much to do, but my father made up his mind that we should get to know each other as soon as possible, so here we are. Love your dress. Has Margaret told you about Miller's in town? We shop there all the time."

"Rach, let the lady catch her breath before you start in with the fashion report for Miller Mercantile," the young man said with a wry smile. "Good evening, I'm Griffin Kelly." He looked at Elizabeth's blue eyes and blonde hair gracefully piled on her head and falling into ringlets down the back, remembering his brother's description of the mysterious woman. How ironic it would be for her to show up this evening. "It's a pleasure. I look forward to a most interesting evening."

Elizabeth was leery of this handsome man who smiled at her as if he knew her darkest secrets. He was tall but with a fairer complexion than Rachel and his father. His build was smaller than Tom Kelly who towered over him as they stood together, and his sandy brown hair was lighter than his sister's. Still, his mischievous grin and easy-going manner made him likable and Elizabeth couldn't help smiling as they talked.

"Actually, I bought this dress at Miller Mercantile and would enjoy comparing...as you say...fashion reports with your sister."

"This is my second son, Griffin," said Tom shooting a stern look at Griff. "My youngest, Lance is spending some time back east with my wife's family. My oldest son was just here. Don't know where he's run off to."

Matt rounded the corner from the kitchen and spotted Elizabeth standing in the parlor. There she was, the woman who haunted his thoughts. What brought her here, he wondered? This couldn't be their dinner guest. He scanned the room for Jack Devlin. Perhaps the gambler had brought her here to plead for the return of the thoroughbred, as if she could change his mind. Matt grumbled to himself and pasted a smile on his face as he headed for the main room. This evening couldn't get over fast enough.

"Ah, here he is," said Tom in a jovial voice. "My oldest son, Matthew."

"Margaret was just introducing us to Mrs. Rogers," said Griffin, jumping in with the introduction as he grinned at his brother. "She's the widow who recently purchased the Butcher ranch and is our new neighbor. Isn't that surprising news?"

"Good evening," Matt said in a dull voice, barely looking at Elizabeth. He scanned the room again, still expecting to see Jack Devlin lurking in a corner with drink in hand, puffing on a cigar. "I didn't realize you were an acquaintance of the Spencers. He repeated that statement in his mind and winced. Of course, she knew the Spencers, he thought. She was heading into Will's office when they collided on the street. Why hadn't he thought to ask Will about her?

Elizabeth's face reddened when she saw Matt. She wanted to hide. How could this be the friendly neighbor Margaret talked about? Had she known this cowboy belonged to the family who owned the Emerald ranch, she never would have come.

"Well, I'm not an acquaintance," she said, glancing at the others. "I mean, we are acquaintances, naturally, but just recently." She laughed nervously, feeling her face flush more.

"What Elizabeth is trying to say is that we had not met before she arrived in town a few days ago, but Will and Elizabeth's uncle have been friends for years. We are just delighted to have her with us in Nevada," said Margaret. She was anxious for the evening to go well and the tension, between these two, young people she thought so much of, was obvious. "Have you two already met?" she questioned.

Elisabeth stood dumbfounded, unsure if she should admit to any encounters she already had with Matt. She waited for him to answer, hoping he would not launch into a summary of their previous disastrous meetings.

"I believe we've run into each other."

Elizabeth looked away and silently sighed with relief. It seemed this man was not interested in admitting to any more than necessary.

"Let's sit down everyone," Tom said, motioning to the others. "Matthew, bring the ladies some wine and something stronger for Will."

Griffin followed his brother to the dining room and watched Matt pour a shot of whiskey, finishing in one gulp as he poured himself another.

"Hey, save some for the rest of us," Griffin said, taking the bottle and pouring his own shot. "It's not that bad. At least you know who she is now and where to find her."

"I thought Reece said she was an old widow. Had I known it was her..."

"That's what we all thought," Griffin laughed. "How many young widows do we know? I don't get you. I thought you liked this woman. She's a pretty girl and single, that would be good enough for me. I'll take her off your hands if you want, with or without shoes."

Griffin drank his shot and poured a second. He enjoyed watching Matt fret. Life came easy for his brother. He was smart, good looking, well respected, and invaluable to their father in running the ranch. Griffin wasn't always taken seriously by his pa and he was jealous of Matt at times.

"No thanks," Matt replied. "One way or another I'm going to have to take care of this one myself." He handed Griffin the bottle of whiskey then picked up the wine in one hand, clasping goblets in the other.

"Are you sure?" said Griff, grabbing four glasses. "Looks like she's already getting the best of you."

"I never let a woman get the best of me. Now, let's go get this night over with."

"The wood trim was fashioned from trees cut right here on the Emerald," Tom explained as they returned to the parlor. "Eleanor, my wife, picked out the carpets and furniture. It took several years to get this place the way she wanted, but worth the work."

Matt stiffly handed a glass to Elizabeth, careful to not make eye contact. She waited as the red wine slowly drained from the bottle, splashing on the bottom of the goblet and raised her finger when she wanted him to stop.

"Thank you," she softly murmured, never lifting her eyes. He turned away and she took a big gulp, discretely touching a handkerchief to her mouth, afterward. If I keep this up, she thought, I'll fall off my chair before dinner. She followed Matt with her eyes as he filled Margaret's glass, and then took another gulp.

"My Rachel has done a good job of taking over the duties of the household in her mother's absence," Tom went on. "She cooks, cleans and takes care of four men. She does it all with a smile on her face, most days. Her mother would be proud."

"We're all proud of her, Tom. She's a fine young lady." said Margaret. She reached out and lightly squeezed Elizabeth's hand. "You two have many things in common and I think you're going to be great friends."

"Well if she's already been to Miller's then I know we're going to get along," said Rachel. "Shopping at Miller Mercantile is payment for putting up with my brothers. Don't let their good manners fool you, Elizabeth. They like to misbehave when my pa isn't around."

Elizabeth smiled and glanced at Matt, catching his eye. She looked away quickly and took another drink of wine. "I had an older brother too," she said. "They do enjoy teasing their sisters."

"That's because little sisters enjoy getting on the nerves of their brother," laughed Griffin. "I think Matt would agree."

Matt smiled slightly. "Little sisters don't mind being teased, even if they squawk about it because they know their brother looks out for them. Isn't that correct, Rachel?"

"Yes," Rachel said, hanging her head with an air of surrender. "Brothers always keep you safe. Even Griff, although I don't like to admit it. She made a face at Griffin who snarled at her in return.

"Behave you two," laughed Margaret. "Elizabeth, I can assure you that all of the Kelly children have been raised with proper manners. Their mother saw to that." She looked at Tom who was grinning proudly, "They inherited their strong work ethic from their father. I've known them all since they were babies and love them as if they were my own. Even when they carry on in front of company."

We're just having fun, Margaret," said Griffin. "Matt, I think Mrs. Rogers needs more wine."

"Elizabeth...please call me Elizabeth," she said, watching Matt refill her glass and thinking she detected a glimmer of a smile when he glanced her way. "My brother teased me all the time when I was young, but he always bought me candy when we went to town. I think he was the best brother a girl ever had."

"See that, Griffin," said Rachel. "I'll expect candy from you in the future. Matt already got me these shoes so it's going to take an awful lot of candy to top that." She raised her dress and wiggled her feet to show off a pair of shiny, black leather shoes. "See what a nice brother he is?"

Elizabeth set her wine glass on the small table next to her chair and slowly stood, mouth gaping, with wide-eyed amazement at Rachel's dancing feet. "Your shoes?" she said. "Those are my shoes."

Rachel looked down at her feet. She turned them from side to side, looking at the toes and then the heels. "These are your shoes?"

"Yes, they are. I bought them before I left. The St. Louis shoe company name is marked on the inside. Why are you wearing my shoes?"

Griffin choked loudly as he swallowed the remaining whiskey in his glass and looked at Matt who was holding his head in his hands like a man just sentenced to death. "Yes Rachel, tell us where you got them?"

"I found them in Matt's room. I thought he bought them for me."

"Why would I buy you a pair of shoes and then keep them in my room?" said Matt lifting his head.

"I don't understand," said Tom looking from face to face for an answer. "If they're your shoes, how did they get in Matthew's room?"

"I forgot them."

"You forgot them in Matt's room?" asked Tom.

"Oh, my," said Margaret. She touched her hand to her chest looking at Elizabeth with a disapproving frown.

"No, it's not like that. I forgot them by the stream because he threw me on the horse."

"I didn't throw you on the horse," said Matt, raising his voice. "I just put you in the saddle and sent you home where you belonged."

"Matthew, what have you done to this young lady," said Tom brusquely, his face reddened with anger.

"He threw me on that horse like I was a sack of potatoes, then slapped the poor animal and scared him, just like he frightened me when he pointed the gun. Of course, all of this was after he tore my dress."

There was a collective gasp in the room and then silence as everyone stared at Matt. He threw up his hands and grunted in complete dismay.

"It's late. Perhaps we should go," Margaret whispered as Will obediently set down his glass and began to rise.

"You pointed your gun at this woman?" Tom roared. "What the devil was going on?"

"No Pa, I pointed it at the snake. She's hysterical as usual."

"As usual?" Rachel asked.

"Well, I must say I'd be hysterical too if someone pointed a gun at me." Margaret eyed Will who obediently sat down again.

"Nobody pointed a gun at her," Matt shouted. "Nobody tore her dress or ruined her hat. If she hadn't been dancing around in the water with her dress in the air I wouldn't have had to pull my gun. Why don't you ask where her gambler friend Jack Devlin was when she almost stepped on a rattler? That's the kind of man she chooses."

Elizabeth stood indignantly and glared at Matt. "What do you mean, that's the kind of man I choose?"

Matt rose from his seat and faced Elizabeth, like a cowboy staring at his enemy before a gunfight. "I saw you prancing around town with him today and I know you both came in on the stage together."

"Prancing?" Elizabeth said, standing her ground.

"I'd be happy to give your shoes back," interrupted Rachel nervously. She began tugging at the shoes to get them off. "This was all a mistake on my part." Her eyes darted around the room at the others. "It's almost time for dinner. I hope you're all hungry."

"More wine, anyone?" asked Griffin with a smirk. "How about another drink, Will? You look like you could use a refill."

Will grinned and stuck out his glass, then settled back in his chair, sipping the whiskey.

"We may have arrived on the same stage, but we did not travel together," said Elizabeth. "He was kind enough to help me compose myself after you plowed me over with that big saddle."

Rachel turned excitedly to Margaret, suddenly remembering the gift from her father. "Pa bought me a new saddle. It's lightweight and so pretty. Much easier for me to ride. I'll have to show you."

"Plowed you over? See, there you go again. I didn't even see you."

Elizabeth sighed loudly and looked at Matt with contempt. "I believe that's the problem. First, you stepped on my dress, which I will admit, was already torn, then you swung that heavy saddle at me, knocking me into Jack Devlin who was, as I've already explained, kind enough to keep me from being trampled as you walked off."

"It really isn't that heavy," said Rachel, "They're actually lightweight compared to a regular one."

"Well had I seen you I would have apologized, I'm sure."

"Oh, you did give me an apology, but it was rushed and certainly not sincere. Now my dress is ruined."

He can buy you a new one," said Griff as he raised his glass to his lips. "He just won seven hundred bucks."

"Shh," said Margaret, putting her finger to her lips. "We're trying to listen." She smiled at the couple who were now aware they had become the evening entertainment. "Go on Matt, I believe it's your turn."

Matt cleared his throat and glanced around at the others who sat mesmerized by the discussion. "Well," he mumbled. "I'm sorry for ruining your dress. Griff's right, I should buy you a new one. You and Rachel can go to Miller's and pick out whatever you like."

The audience exhaled and smiled at one another, pleased with themselves as well as Matt and the tension in the room began to subside.

Elizabeth's face softened, and she smiled shyly at Matt. "I don't want you to buy me a dress. I told you it was already torn." She paused for a moment. "I was hoping we would run into each other again because I wanted to thank you for the other day when you saved my life. I wasn't nice to you afterward and I'm sorry."

"You were right, I should have warned you before I pulled my gun, but if I had, you might have screamed, and the snake would have lunged for you. I did what I thought was best."

"No, I see now, you were right, I probably would have screamed. I should have trusted you. It seems like I've made a mess of a lot of things since I arrived."

"So, does that mean you'll stay for dinner? Rachel's worked hard all day. She's been excited about meeting you. Even if you don't like me, don't judge my family because of the way I've acted."

"Of course, I'll stay for dinner. Margaret and Will have been so complimentary about all of you. I like your family and I don't see how I could resist."

"Well, now that that's all settled, let's eat," said Griff. "I've been smelling that food for the last hour. Margaret, shall we lead the way?" He rose and offered his arm and she shook her head and laughed. "Griffin, you are always a delight."

"Can we call a truce?" asked Matt.

Elizabeth timidly placed her hand around Matt's arm and followed the others into the dining room, looking at him closely for the first time. There was strength in this man who enveloped her as they walked, as if nothing bad could touch her, as long as she was in his care. The tenderness in his voice was soothing and when he smiled at her, everyone else in the room seemed to disappear. She wondered how she hadn't noticed before.

The trip home at the end of the evening seemed short. Isn't it curious how things turned out, she thought? A man she dislikes so much in the morning is the same man she enjoys so much in the evening. What a wonderful evening it was, too. Her head was whirling from the food and wine and conversation.

"Did you enjoy yourself?" asked Margaret as they rode in the buggy.

"Yes, it was very nice," laughed Elizabeth, "once we resolved the ownership of the shoes. I think the Kelly family will be fine neighbors."

"They are an extraordinary family," said Margaret. "Matt is a handsome young man. I can't think of one girl who hasn't had her eye on him at one time or another. He's quite a catch in my book." She gazed at Will and squeezed his arm. "Of course, I already have my handsome man."

"Is Matt courting anyone now?" Elizabeth asked, suddenly afraid he might be taken.

"No one that I've heard about. He's very particular about the young ladies he sees. I hope you have an opportunity to spend more time together."

Will looked at Margaret and winked, but Elizabeth didn't notice. Her thoughts were still on the Emerald ranch and the feeling of happiness she hadn't experienced in a long time.

CHAPTER 9

THE NIGHT VISITOR

Elizabeth pouted as she held the dress in front of her and looked in the mirror. The church bazaar was today, and she couldn't decide what to wear. She threw the dress on the pile with the others, sulking over her dilemma.

Why did she let Margaret talk her in to this? She told the Spencers when she arrived that she wanted to concentrate on ranching. She was busy with her garden, spending hours hoeing rows, planting seeds, carrying water. Her plants were just beginning to sprout and needed care.

With a critical eye, Elizabeth sifted through the pile of clothes laying on the bed. She was too frugal to buy something new so soon after the shoes and dress from Miller's which left her with no choice but to wear something she already had. She pulled a red dress from the bottom of the stack, imagining what it might look like with different buttons and a new collar, nodding to herself in approval.

Margaret was right when she advised her to meet more people and church was the best place to start. The garden club ladies were anxious for an introduction and it seemed every woman in town was a member. Elizabeth didn't have a thing to contribute for the bazaar. The other women had a head start. They canned vegetables, sewed quilts and preserved jams. Baking was out of the question. According to Margaret, a member of the club was known for her pies with a crust so flaky the other women never bothered to compete. Of course, everything was to raise money for charity, but what could she add to the sale? Her solution was a simple childhood treat she use to make with her mother. Just some sugar water and string and Elizabeth would have rock candy. It was a great idea, she thought, and took only a couple of days to prepare. The garden club had nothing on her.

Luke volunteered to be her escort for the day along with Henry. Their relationship had warmed since the trip to town when he expressed his opinion of Jack Devlin. The two settled into a conversation each morning over breakfast where Henry, although sometimes begrudgingly, filled Elizabeth in on the progress of the ranch. She was impressed with his knowledge and realized the benefits of listening and learning from his experience. She hinted about going along on the cattle drive in the spring, but Henry had ignored her so far. She wondered if a woman on a trail drive was considered as unlucky as a woman on a ship and might produce a mutiny among the other cowboys. Women never did anything exciting and after all, it was her ranch and her cattle. She was hoping Luke could soften Henry up about letting her go.

Luke had become a true friend. When she returned from the Kelly ranch carrying her shoes, she confided that Matt Kelly was the cowboy antagonist she kept running into. She chattered on about the Emerald and the Kelly family, describing each one as if Luke had never seen them. Tom Kelly was well known and both Luke and Henry had been around him and his family for many years. Matt and Griffin were fine young men in his opinion.

Rachel had grown into a young woman as beautiful and smart as her mother. They had a good laugh over the discovery of the shoes in the possession of Rachel. It was one of those situations in life that seems like a disaster at the time but is actually quite amusing in retrospect.

The task of replacing old buttons with black ones worked well on the red dress and black lace for the collar added the right touch. She was pleased with what she saw when she took a last look in the mirror before climbing in the wagon.

"Elizabeth." She heard her name called and turned to see Rachel Kelly waving. "Margaret told me you were coming so I've been on the lookout. It can be daunting when you don't know anyone. What did you bring for the bake sale?"

"Rock candy," Elizabeth answered somewhat embarrassed when she saw the other choices. There was an entire table devoted to cakes which Rachel explained were set aside for a cake walk.

"Wish I'd thought of that," said Rachel. "I bring the same thing every year. A plate of cookies that are my secret recipe. They're Griff's favorite. He always buys the whole plate. I guess Margaret told you about Mrs. Bernard's apply pie. People are already lining up for a piece. Let me introduce you around."

"There's Griff with his latest love interest, Clara Richter. She's a bit clingy and a snob. Her father owns the mill so naturally she likes to flaunt that. I don't know what he sees in her. She's not his type if you ask me. You can meet her later."

"Mrs. Miller is the gray-haired woman standing by the church next to Mrs. Ferguson. You probably met Mr. Ferguson, the bank president. Their son Bart is around here some place. He asked to take me home."

She suddenly grabbed Elizabeth's arm and stopped, looking like she just saw something gruesome. "Quick, turn around and pretend like you don't see him," she said. "It's Toby Elliot." She gave a cross-eyed look at Elizabeth and dragged her along as they started to walk back to the food table. "He follows all the girls around. His mother treats him like he's twelve and is always pushing him on us. I try my best to avoid him."

"Rachel, there you are. I've been waiting for you."

"Too late," Rachel said and turned back around still holding on to Elizabeth who wanted to laugh as a roly-poly young man ran toward them, waving. He was disheveled with his shirt tail partially pulled out and bow tie leaning to one side. His dark hair was plastered to his head and parted in the middle. He looked like a young boy in a man's body.

"Mother said you would come." He stopped to catch his breath before examining Elizabeth with beady eyes and a sly smile. "Who's your friend?"

Rachel was right. He was odd and made Elizabeth uncomfortable when he looked at her. She hoped their conversation would be short and could see why young women tried to avoid him. He reminded her of Jacob Biggs from back home.

"This is Elizabeth Rogers, newly arrived from St. Louis. She bought the Butcher ranch and is very busy," answered Rachel in a monotone voice.

"The Butcher ranch? My mother heard someone moved in. I'll call on you tomorrow and we can go for a ride," the roly-poly man said.

"Well..." A flustered Elizabeth stumbled over words as she looked to Rachel with fear in her eyes."

"I told you Toby, she doesn't go out much," said Rachel. "She's a grieving widow."

"All the same, I will call on you," Toby insisted as a giant hand came down on his shoulder, pinching so hard he grimaced and tried to pull away, looking like he might break out in tears.

"Toby," said the serious man with a firm grip. "How about going over to the baked goods table and getting yourself a big slice of apple pie. You tell the ladies I'll be over in a couple of minutes to pay for it."

"But sheriff, I was talking to Rachel and her friend. I was about to ask them..."

"Now, come on Toby," said the sheriff. "You're not going to turn down a piece of Mary Bernard's pie? Besides, the little Kelly sister and this pretty young lady have previous plans. They don't have the time to talk with you. Tell Mrs. Bernard to make it a big ol' piece."

Toby Elliott excused himself and scurried off toward the pie line leaving the two women to exhale in a sigh of relief as Sheriff Cameron stood grinning.

"Stop calling me that," Rachel said in frustration as she hit the sheriff in the arm with her purse. "I told you I'm not a little girl anymore and you can't say those things to people. She looked annoyed at the sheriff who acted wounded and held his arm in pretend pain.

"You pack a wallop in that punch. Shame on you for beatin' up the local law. I may have to complain to your daddy," said the sheriff with a flash of blue eyes in the direction of Elizabeth. "Who's this young lady?"

"Elizabeth Rogers. Just moved into the Butcher place and you're not going to tell my pa anything, Reece. I'll turn my brothers on you."

"How you going to do that Rach? Griff is over there spooning with Clara. Lance is clear across the country and Matt is hauling some bull back from down south," the sheriff said chuckling. "Besides, you should be happy I'm here to protect you from the likes of Toby Elliott." He turned to Elizabeth again and tipped his hat. "Ma'am, I'm Reece Cameron, the sheriff. Pleased to make your acquaintance and don't let Rachel taint your opinion of me. I'm a very lovable guy."

Elizabeth giggled as she watched the two sparing. "I'm not taking sides Sheriff Cameron. I wouldn't want to get in trouble with the law and Rachel is a friend. I take it you two have known each other for a while?"

"Since she was a little thing following me and Griff around where ever we went," said Reece. "She may have grown up, but I have to keep her in her place when she gets a little too sassy. What are you two pretty girls up to today?"

"I was showing Elizabeth around and then I'm off to find Bart Ferguson," answered Rachel. "He promised to take me home and he says he loves my cookies, so he may be buying them all before Griff does. Would you mind escorting Elizabeth over to the garden club table? I think Margaret is there. I see Bart is waiting by the horses and he might be wondering where I am."

"If he's over by the horses with that bunch, he's probably doing something he shouldn't. You be careful riding home with him," said Reece. "Come get me if you need. In the meantime, I'd be happy to take this young lady anywhere she wants to go."

"Oh Reece, you're such an old man sometimes," said Rachel. "I'll bring Bart over and introduce him later, Elizabeth." She turned and walked toward the group of young men gathered by a string of horses, leaving Elizabeth with Sheriff Cameron.

"So, you're the widow who bought the Butcher place?" said Reece. "You're not exactly what we were expecting."

"I got that feeling when I had dinner at the Kelly ranch," Elizabeth laughed. "It was quite a shock to them. Did you say Matt was out of town?"

Reece looked perplexed for a moment. Matt's luck from the card game was holding out if he caught the interest of this woman, thought Reece. He must have made a good impression at dinner. "Yeah, he's been gone a couple of days. I guess he didn't make it back in time for the bazaar. He's usually the one in charge of watching out for Rachel."

"I didn't realize she needed watching out for," said Elizabeth. "Rachel seems to do alright by herself." She was a little put out by Reece's comment.

"Tom wants to make sure she's not running wild and it's generally up to Matt and Griff to see that doesn't happen. I mean, she's a good kid and all, but I like to keep track of who she's with."

"I believe that was part of the conversation at their dinner," Elizabeth replied. "That brothers tend to watch out for their younger sisters. It's probably a comfort to her even if she doesn't want to admit it."

"How was dinner?" chuckled Reece. "Did she make those cookies?"

"It was all delicious, but no cookies. She did have a wonderful chocolate cake for dessert. If you're talking about the ones made from her secret recipe they must be good. Griffin buys them every year."

Well, about that," Reece laughed. "Those cookies are awful. We all know it, but she's so proud of them none of us have the heart to tell her."

"Sheriff," Elizabeth exclaimed.

"Hey, I speak the truth," said Reece. "Griffin buys them every year because he doesn't want anyone complaining. Most of the time he throws them in the weeds. The parson found a dead coyote out back of the church last year after the bazaar. Griff and I were sure the poor thing had eaten Rachel's cookies."

"That's terrible," Elizabeth laughed. "She's bound to find out one of these days."

"Not if you don't tell her. Bart Ferguson is in for a surprise if he eats them. Do me a favor and tell Margaret to hide them until Griff has time to get over there. I think I'll go see what's going on by the horses."

Elizabeth watched the sheriff walk away thinking what a good man he must be. She was glad he mentioned Matt. She was disappointed he hadn't contacted her but at least now she knew he was out of town and that knowledge gave her hope she might see him in the future.

Jack Devlin was nowhere to be found either so Elizabeth felt abandoned by both men. Of course, it was no surprise if Jack decided to go on to Sacramento since that was his original plan. Still, she hoped she might have a chance to say goodbye.

"Margaret, the sheriff wants you to put Rachel's cookies aside for Griffin," Elizabeth said as she approached the baked sale table. She smiled at the other ladies of the garden club and inspected the table of food. "Everything looks so good, I may end up taking it all home."

"I've already hidden the cookies," Margaret whispered, giving Elizabeth a hug. "I'm so glad you came. You look wonderful in that dress."

Elizabeth beamed as she was introduced to the other members and took her spot behind the table. Her job was to cut pieces of pie. She was amazed at the line of people ready to buy their choice of apple or rhubarb.

"Mrs. Bernard, you must spend days preparing all these," she said in amazement. "I don't know how you do it."

"I've done it for so many years, I have a whole routine down now and Juanita Miller is a good helper. I couldn't do it without her," Mary Bernard replied. "Of course, I'm always scared I'll confuse my pies with my hats and what a fiasco that would be."

"Your hats?"

"Yes, I own the millinery," said Mary. "Can you imagine if I attached a piece of rhubarb to a hat and baked a ribbon in my pie?" She chuckled and handed a slice to a young boy."

"And some rock candy, too," said the boy as he handed his money to Mrs. Bernard and grabbed a string of the candy before running off with his mouth full of pie.

"Your candy has certainly been a hit. I think every boy here has bought at least one piece," said Mary. "We're so proud to have you do this for such a good cause. The parson was asking about you."

"Miss Elizabeth, I was wondering if you would like to participate in the cake walk with me. Mother said she would pay for the tickets and it's about to start."

Elizabeth looked up to see Toby Elliott standing by the table, googling with his beady eyes and smudge of chocolate on his shirt collar. "Well, thank you for asking Toby but I'm afraid I have to work my share of time." She managed a faint smile and resumed her work of cutting pies.

"Mother said she would be happy to take over for you," answered Toby. "I have the money for the tickets here." He dug in his pants pocket and pulled out crumpled bills.

"I think Rachel told you that I'm a grieving widow," answered Elizabeth, ashamed of the lie. "I'm sure you'll find another lady who would be interested in the cake walk."

"May I take you home then?" insisted Toby. "I've already spoken to Henry and he agreed if you were willing."

"Oh, I couldn't have you take me home." Elizabeth was shocked this man would be so bold as to speak with Henry without consulting her first. She was taught to be friendly to everyone, but Toby had gone too far. Who did he think he was?

"You're too late, Toby. This lady already promised to let me take her home. In fact, she has no further use for your attentions which means I better not see you bothering her again. Do you understand?"

Someone softly touched Elizabeth's arm, taking it in hand and pulling her close and for a moment she was relieved the sheriff had returned to rescue her, but when she looked up, she saw the face of Matt Kelly.

"Isn't that right, Mrs. Rogers?"

Her worries melted away and she smiled back like an infatuated school girl unable to speak. "Yes," she finally answered. "Yes, I did."

"Did I keep you waiting long? I hurried as fast as I could."

"Not long, but it doesn't matter, you're here now," she said in a dreamy voice. "Toby was asking about a cake walk."

"I heard, but I'd much rather walk with you than a cake. Let's go find Henry and remind him I was to take you home."

"I'm cutting pies."

Matt pulled out a crisp bill and handed it to Mary Bernard. "You don't mind if she leaves her post early, do you Mary? This ought to cover a big chunk of chocolate cake for Toby and make up for any time missed." He smiled at Elizabeth once more, wrapped her hand around his arm and led her away from the table. "Are you hungry? The Elkhorn Saloon is selling food."

"I thought you were in Texas?" Elizabeth asked as she watched Matt scoop up a plate of ham and beans. Her heart was fluttering from being near him and she couldn't eat a bite.

"I was and wanted to get back sooner but that bull Pa bought has a mind of its own. I thought I might miss the whole thing. I had a hunch you'd be here. I saw Henry with a group of men, earlier. We can go find him when I'm finished."

Henry stared with his usual stern face when he saw Elizabeth with Matt. "You seem to have more than your share of men wanting to drive you home," he said. "I told that other fellow I was the one who brought you and I'd be taking you home, but seeing how it's Matt, then I guess it'll be alright."

"Toby told me you gave him permission to take me home?" said Elizabeth. "Without my approval?"

"Toby Elliott is a weasel and will say anything," said Matt "Henry has a right to be concerned. He's just trying to look out for your welfare. He took Elizabeth's arm and guided her away from the crowd. "My buggy is this way, over by the horses."

The pink sunset painted with graying clouds hovered in the distance offering a serene background on the ride home. Matt and Elizabeth sat in silence, admiring the landscape. Between the gentle swaying of the buggy and methodical clip clop of horse hooves, Elizabeth was growing sleepy and her mouth opened in a yawn. She giggled as a tiny squeak emerged.

"I'm sorry," she laughed." "It's not the company at all. I guess I'm more tired than I thought. I was up early."

"I take no offense," Matt said with a grin. "Actually, this buggy ride made me realize it's been a long day. I pushed hard to get back because I was hoping to see you. I guess Margaret told you she and Will are having a get-together tomorrow night?"

"Yes, she's determined to keep me busy, although I must admit I've had a fun time on each occasion."

"Even the Kelly catastrophe?" Matt laughed

"Especially at the Kelly dinner. I'm glad we finally met on friendly terms. Elizabeth smiled shyly and looked away trying to hide a second yawn.

"I'm hoping you'll let me escort you. When Margaret puts her mind to something it's hard to stop her and she is determined that you know everyone in town. The Spencers love to entertain and if you let me take you, we can make a quick getaway if it becomes overwhelming. That is, if it's alright with Henry."

"He let you bring me home tonight so I'm sure I can talk him into it," said Elizabeth laughing with excitement. "I'm looking forward to it."

When they arrived at the ranch, the two lingered on the porch talking until they heard the wagon carrying Henry and Luke rattling up to the barn. "I should probably go in now," Elizabeth said quietly. "It's getting late."

Matt put his arms around her waist and bent down to kiss her when he heard a voice behind him. "Getting ready to go home, Matt? It's late and I wouldn't want you to get lost in the dark."

He turned around to find Henry leaning against the porch railing with a determined look that said it was time to go. He'd seen that look from fathers in the past.

"Evening Henry, I was just saying goodnight to Elizabeth."

"Well say it and be done." Henry didn't budge from where he stood.

Turning back to Elizabeth she blushed and giggled with embarrassment. He winked as he held her hand and bid her goodnight. She watched him climb in the buggy and drive away before going into the house and up the stairs to bed.

Elizabeth sat in a rocker in front of an open window, partially dressed, brushing her hair. The breeze was cool on her skin and she closed her eyes, listening to the sound of cicadas outside. It was a wonderful day and she replayed the conversations with Matt in her head. Her only concern now was the need for another new dress. The red one worked well but she would have to sift through the armoire tomorrow to find another. It had to be a special dress, because Matt would be her escort. She wondered how wise it was to make a return trip to Miller Mercantile and if she could get Henry or Luke to take her to town. She knew Henry wasn't the type to understand the importance of a new dress, but Luke could be persuaded.

The clicking insects gave way to the sound of rustling bushes outside her bedroom window. Elizabeth sat motionless, brush paused midway through her hair and listened. Her room was dark, and the moon cast its light over the ground. She saw nothing as she held her breath wondering if the breeze was responsible for the noise. The cicadas resumed their clatter, but something caused her to tense up and squeeze the arm of the rocker. She caught sight of a figure, dressed in dark clothing emerge from the shadows, running through the yard in the darkness.

"Henry," she screamed, grabbing a robe and running down the stairs in her bare feet, tripping over the dragging tie belt and falling to the floor when she reached the bottom. She rose and continued to run when she heard a gunshot. "Henry," she screamed again, throwing open the door and running out to the porch.

The light from a swinging lantern moved in the distance. "Get back in the house and lock the door," Henry's gruff voice called out. "Don't open it until I come back."

Elizabeth slammed the front door and locked it behind her. She bolted for the stairs, climbing two at a time, shut the window with a bang and locking it tightly, ran to the corner of the room where she sat on the floor holding her knees tight against her chest, listening to sounds of shouting outside. Minutes ticked away as she sat in the dark waiting to hear from Henry. A hard knock at the front door and the sound of him calling her name, drew her downstairs again.

"Open up, Elizabeth. It's me."

She timidly unlocked the door, opening it a crack to peer outside. Henry stood, shotgun in hand peeking back at her. "You alright in there?"

"Yes," she said, opening the door wide enough for him to step inside. "What happened? I saw a man outside my window and heard shooting." Elizabeth was visibly shaken, and Henry gave her a hug that, she was sure, might squeeze the life out of her.

"We don't know who it was. We just settled down in the bunk house when Luke noticed something moving outside and saw someone running around the corner by the house. It better not be that Elliot boy, or I'll fill his backside with buckshot if I see him again."

"Don't be silly, Henry," replied Elizabeth. "Toby Elliott couldn't run that fast, if you were a step behind him ready to shoot. I saw the figure from my window and the man was taller and slender." She cast her eyes downward, trembling as she thought of the man staring up at her sitting in the rocker. "What do you suppose he wanted?"

"Hard to say." Henry knew the conversation was frightening Elizabeth and had to admit he was puzzled by the whole thing. "Luke followed the man as far as he could but wasn't able to keep up. He got a shot off before losing him in the dark. I think we need to pay a visit to Sheriff Cameron tomorrow morning, but until then, I'll sleep here on the sofa for tonight."

"If it's alright, I think I'll sleep on the floor next to you." Elizabeth stood there shaking, not wanting to go to her room.

"Tell you what." Henry suddenly noticed Elizabeth's open robe and looked away, embarrassed. "Why don't you go put on something else and come out to the bunk house with me and Luke? We'll all sleep better if you do."

Elizabeth grinned and ran upstairs to change while Henry waited, insisting he search inside for anything suspicious. She hovered close beside him as they walked to the bunk house where Luke was waiting, knowing if she slept at all it would be under the protection of the two men.

CHAPTER 10

SHOTS IN THE DARK

Reece Cameron listened to Elizabeth's description of the night visitor seen sneaking around her ranch with less enthusiasm than expected. She and Henry made an early trip into town to talk with the sheriff about the unknown man and the footsteps they found under her window as well as near the barn and by the road, but Reece claimed there was nothing he could do.

"It's not that I'm not concerned, Henry," Reece said. "You know the safety of women in this town is important to me, but I can't go around arresting every tall, thin man dressed in black as a suspect. My jail cells would be spilling over. Without more to go on, the only thing to do is to keep Elizabeth in your sights and make sure the doors and windows are locked. It would probably be prudent to close the curtains," Reece added, with a look of wry amusement. "A lady in her night clothes can attract the interest of most people passing by."

"This is not a joke." Henry's face contorted in anger as he lashed out in response to the sheriff's comment. "This young lady has a right to live in her home without fear and, I daresay, unmolested..."

"Henry, please," said Elizabeth, embarrassed at his remarks.

"I'm sorry, Elizabeth," Henry replied, calming down after taking a deep breath. "I'll not stand here and let the sheriff take this lightly. If there's a man sneaking around that ranch after you or anything else, then he'll find a loaded shotgun waiting for him."

"Henry, I am not taking this lightly," Reece answered abashed. He glanced at Elizabeth apologetically. "And I mean to catch the culprit. I realize that she has a right to do whatever she wants but Elizabeth is a pretty woman, and, in my experience, pretty women attract men and some of them don't have good manners or good sense for that matter. All I'm asking is that she takes a few precautions."

"That's more like it," Henry grumbled. "Now, you let me know if you find anything suspicious and, in the meantime, I'll take Elizabeth over to Miller's. It seems she needs to buy a dress for some party the Spencers are having tonight, although if you ask me she's got a stack of them already."

"Henry," Elizabeth cried out in agony. She looked helplessly at Reece and blushed. She was pleased Henry agreed to make a stop at Miller's but after the conversation with Reece about her appearance at the window last night, she wasn't prepared for a lecture about the number of dresses she owned. The sheriff was amused enough at her expense and she felt it was time to go.

Reece grinned at Elizabeth and tipped his hat. "You have a nice day shopping ma'am, and don't you worry, I'll get this straightened out. Do you have someone who can get you to this party safely?"

"Matt Kelly is my escort."

"Then you'll be in good hands."

Henry left Elizabeth at Miller's while he met with Will Spencer about the ranch. Elizabeth presumed it was to discuss the late-night visitor and not the profitability of her investment. Henry felt the weight of responsibility for her fell on his shoulders even though, as far as she was concerned, she was responsible for her own welfare.

She was a little surprised he stood up for her in the sheriff's office. It was more than just a duty to the job. He was genuinely concerned for her and perturbed with Sheriff Cameron's attitude. Elizabeth couldn't imagine anyone else doing a better job of putting the sheriff in his place. She felt indebted to Henry for a reason she couldn't explain and wanted to repay him but had no idea how to go about it. She decided to write her uncle for advice.

Juanita Miller was delighted to see Elizabeth and whisked her to the back of the store to show off the newest selection of dresses that arrived from San Francisco. Elizabeth loved Juanita's exuberant personality. She was a stocky woman in her fifties or pleasantly plump and young at heart as Juanita liked to say. She loved fashion and her graying hair, worn in a bun, was always adorned in ornate hairpins to match the latest styles she wore.

"Ruffles are the rage in Paris," she said, pointing out a dress made of blue satin, trimmed in black. "When Mr. Miller and I went to San Francisco last month, that's all they talked about. Lots of ruffles...and layers, of course. Everything nowadays has layers."

She held the dress next to Elizabeth, humming as she pinched and tightened it around Elizabeth's body then rested her chin in her hand, deep in thought. "It's perfect," Juanita declared. "With your hair and eye color, you'll look like a dream."

"I don't know," said Elizabeth, hesitating. "It's more expensive than the other things I own. Are you sure this is the right sort of thing for Margaret's party?"

"Absolutely, my dear." replied Mrs. Miller throwing her hands in the air dramatically. "I wish I had your figure. There won't be a man who can keep his eyes off you when you walk in. Rachel Kelly would die for this dress, but of course you saw it first."

Elizabeth stood for a moment, scrutinizing the dress. She didn't care if every man at the party kept their eyes on her. She was only interested in one pair of eyes and those belonged to Matt Kelly and if Mrs. Miller said this dress would do the trick then it was the dress she wanted.

Henry grumbled as he put the large box in the wagon, wondering why such a small woman would need such a big package. "How many do you have in here? I thought you were just buying one."

"There's only one," Elizabeth laughed. "I don't want it to wrinkle before tonight and it's delicate. Mrs. Miller said it would be safer in the bigger box." She was excited about the evening and being with Matt again and suddenly reached over and kissed Henry on the cheek. "Thank you for bringing me to town and worrying about me. I realize you don't always approve of the things I do but I believe your heart is in the right place."

Henry stood for a moment staring at the back of the wagon, unable to look Elizabeth in the eyes. He rearranged the dress box and glanced back toward Miller's then cleared his throat finally able to speak.

"Now don't go making a fuss. I told you before, it's my responsibility to keep you out of trouble. Will Spencer would be on a rampage if I didn't take care of you." He looked humbly at Elizabeth and smiled awkwardly as if mustering a pleasant face hadn't been tried in years. "Just don't go thinking I'm going to haul you to town every time some young man comes knocking at the door. I've got my work to do, you know."

"I know," Elizabeth said and smiled as she climbed in the wagon for the ride home. She knew Henry was not the type to show emotion, especially for someone he thought as silly as her. Still, it was nice to see that touch of a smile and she hoped she'd be able to coax another from him again.

Matt's ear to ear grin as Elizabeth floated down the stairs confirmed the dress was perfect and so was she. "I've never seen your blue eyes shine brighter," he said. "You look like a princess from one of Rachel's story books. There won't be a man there who isn't envious of me."

"Stop or this will all go to my head," Elizabeth laughed. "Although I have to admit I'm enjoying the attention. You're quite charming when you're not stepping on my feet."

"Then you don't want me as a dance partner."

Elizabeth thought of Alex with compunction as Matt helped her into the buggy. She wondered if he would approve of all of this. Her life had changed in the short time since moving west and she felt herself growing further and further away from who she was before. Her desire to be a successful rancher conflicted at times with the lifestyle she now had. Both things brought her happiness. She felt there was time for socializing as well as working and had no desire to compromise on either.

Will took her arm from Matt when they arrived at the Spencer home, pleased to introduce her to their other guests. Margaret teased earlier that this would be her coming-out party and it certainly seemed that way. The Spencers liked to entertain and no one could do it better than Margaret. Their already beautiful home was immaculate and arranged with tables adorned in fine linens, displaying finger foods and punch for their company. Several hired women served champagne and a pianist sat playing at the baby grand piano in the parlor. If the governor himself walked in, Elizabeth couldn't be any more surprised.

She knew many of the other guests already. The Fergusons, Millers and Mary Bernard all complimented her on her appearance. "Juanita told me about your dress. I have a hat that will be the perfect accent," Mary whispered.

"I hope you're not still mad at me from this morning." Elizabeth turned around, surprised the see Sheriff Cameron standing behind her. "It's good to know Matt got you here safely."

"Elizabeth, do you know Reece Cameron, our sheriff? He's a friend of mine from way back," said Matt.

"Yes, we met this morning in his office."

"Really?" said Matt with a dubious smile. "What were you doing in Reece's office?"

Elizabeth hesitated not wanting to rehash the events from last night with Matt or anyone else at the party. She looked sternly at Reece in an attempt to discourage him from launching into a detailed explanation, but he ignored her.

"Mrs. Rogers had some trouble out at her place," Reece began. "A prowler, sneaking around her ranch obviously up to no good. Henry brought her in this morning. I didn't handle things very professionally and I'm afraid she left somewhat upset about the whole thing."

"Why wasn't I told about this?" asked Matt. "What exactly happened? Were you hurt?"

Elizabeth was disgusted with the sheriff for involving Matt and made it clear she did not appreciate his continued discussion of the incident. If he told Matt she was only dressed in camisole and petticoat, Elizabeth would box his ears right there in front of everyone."

"I believe Mrs. Rogers was uninjured and safe in her bedroom at the time," said Reece giving Elizabeth an understanding look that meant he knew he would suffer her wrath if he told Matt the whole story. "Henry and Luke saw him running outside and tried to chase him down but he got away. They found footprints by the barn and a few other places and horse tracks by the road."

The sheriff smiled at Elizabeth, checking to see if his explanation was satisfactory to her. "I told Henry there isn't much we can do without a better description but it's understandable that the lady would be concerned."

"It's odd that you mentioned all of this. I had the strangest feeling of being followed on my way home last night. I can't put my finger on why, but I just got that feeling there was someone else around. I kept looking behind me but never saw a thing." Matt took Elizabeth's hands in his, speaking quietly. "I wish you would have confided in me."

"Elizabeth, our town hasn't been too welcoming so far," said Reece, apologetically. "Will told me you had a run-in with a cowboy on the street outside his office the day you arrived. I'm still trying to figure out who that was. Probably someone passing through. I keep a pretty close lookout for the wild ones. I don't want to see my town get a bad reputation."

Elizabeth and Matt looked at each other and laughed. She blushed as their eyes met, feeling foolish for having ever complained to Will. "That problem was resolved sheriff. I believe I misjudged the situation. Your town has been nothing but considerate and I have no complaints."

"Actually, that was me, Reece," laughed Matt. "I was not my usual kind-hearted self that day."

"How long have you two known each other? Did you tell her about winning the horse from that gambler?" Reece realized Matt and Elizabeth were not just passing acquaintances and made a mental note to ask Griff to fill him in on the background. "It was quite a game. Never saw a man get so lucky. Discarded a queen of hearts and came up with a seven. Betting on an inside straight took a lot of guts."

"What horse? What gambler? You don't mean you won Jack Devlin's horse in a card game? He never mentioned that to me. He said he was in town on business for several days."

"Yes, I won his horse and seven hundred dollars on top of that. When did he tell you he was staying?" said Matt, perturbed at the mention of Devlin's name. "I thought he was leaving for Sacramento right after he turned over the horse which was the day I saw you two together walking down the street."

"So, Jack Devlin has been escorting you around town as well as Matt?" Reece wished he hadn't mentioned the gambler or card game. He hadn't realized it was a sore subject and could feel the tension building between the two. This is what I get for opening my mouth, he thought. He was even more intrigued with their relationship and quite interested in talking to Griffin. He had never seen Matt so emotional over a female. It was quite humorous, and he knew Griff would tell him all the details."

"No, he has not been escorting me around town, although someone can't seem to get that out of his head," Elizabeth said in a huff, directing her animosity at Matt. "I've said several times that we just happened to come in on the same stage and we happened to run into each other when I was in town."

"He's just staying to make trouble, I'm sure of it," said Matt. "I wouldn't be surprised if he was the one sneaking around your ranch last night. He always dresses in black."

"Not tonight," said Reece, casually. "He's been sitting over in the corner by himself since I got here. I heard he's doing business with Will now. Devlin wants him to handle some investments and stopped in to see Will this week. He seems friendly enough to me."

They looked casually toward the corner where Jack Devlin sat smoking a cigar. He wore a white linen suit with ruffled shirt and raised his glass in a toast when he saw the three staring. They all turned around quickly. Ruffles are the rage, thought Elizabeth looking at his shirt and remembering Juanita Miller's comment.

Reece started to chuckle. "You think he saw us."

"He's coming over," Matt answered looking again out of the corner of his eye. He was vexed at the situation and tried to think of an excuse to guide Elizabeth away from the approaching gambler. He saw Griffin standing in the corner with Clara Richter and grabbed Elizabeth's arm hoping to get away before Devlin caught up, but Jack spoke before she could be moved.

"Mrs. Rogers, you look beautiful as always. I hope you haven't forgotten your promise to have lunch with me."

Elizabeth couldn't help smiling despite knowing it irked Matt. Jack was a friend and she wouldn't deny it. Besides, she was pleased to see him and if it meant she and Matt would be at odds, she would have to take that chance.

"We were just talking about you Jack," said Elizabeth. "There was some discussion about whether or not you were still in town. I understand you have already met these two gentlemen."

Jack maintained his smile for Elizabeth although he despised seeing her with Matt Kelly. He regretted that this young lady found Matt interesting and noticed Matt putting his arm around her waist as a show of ownership. He had hoped to enjoy her company himself for his duration in town.

"Yes, we had an interesting meeting at the Elkhorn where this gentleman skillfully won possession of something dear to me," he said leering at Matt. "I'm hoping he'll give me a chance to win my fine horse back in another game. It would be the gentlemanly thing to do. I met a charming young woman whose name is also Kelly, earlier this evening. I believe the Spencers have gathered the prettiest ladies in town," he continued with a wry smile as he kissed Elizabeth's hand while watching Matt from the corner of his eye. "But of course, you are the prettiest of them all."

Matt looked at Griffin again wondering how he could get away from this conversation with Devlin. "I'm afraid I don't have much time for poker and the gentlemanly thing to do is accept your loss. I thought you were leaving town?"

"Not while I have unfinished business. I don't give up easily Mr. Kelly so I'm sure we'll meet again before my stay is over. Now, if you will excuse me, I need to bid farewell to our hosts and thank them again for their hospitality. I have a previously scheduled appointment for later this evening and sadly, will not be able to remain and enjoy Elizabeth's delightful company."

"Isn't Jack Devlin handsome?" said Rachel, approaching the group as the gambler crossed the room toward Will. "I just love the way he talks."

Reece looked at Matt and rolled his eyes at Rachel's giddy laugh. "He's so polite and his accent just makes me melt. I didn't realize you won his horse. It's so awful for him. He loves that animal so much. Matt, you should sell the horse back to him. He says he would be so grateful and what are you going to do with a racehorse anyway?" She turned to watch Devlin walk out the door. "The only thing he talked about was Elizabeth and that horse. He spoke highly of you."

Matt's face reddened and inflated with anger, looking like his head might explode at any moment as he stood staring with a malicious grimace toward the door. His grip tightened around Elizabeth's waist so hard she gave out a small yelp and thought for sure she would be bruised tomorrow. Devlin was apparently trying to use Rachel to convince him to sell the horse and it wasn't going to work.

"What's wrong with him?" Rachel asked, astounded at her brother's reaction.

Reece put his arm around her shoulder and shook his head as he looked down at Rachel's surprised expression. "I don't think your brother shares your high opinion of Jack Devlin. He will burn in… let's just say it will take a miracle before he sells that horse. It's a matter of principle now and his honor is at stake." He gave Rachel a quick hug and chuckled. "You'd understand these things if you were a man. Now, why don't you and I mosey on over and talk to Griff and Miss Snooty Hooty and leave these two alone."

"Like I don't understand a thing about men," said Rachel sarcastically as she elbowed the sheriff. "I don't want to talk to Clara. She's such a bore with 'My daddy owns this, and my daddy owns that.' It's nauseating." `

"Come on, it'll be fun. Besides, your daddy owns 'this and that' too so she's got nothing on you. Why do you think she keeps such a tight grip on your brother? He probably needs a break from her by now." Reece took her arm and led her away despite her protest. "Where's that new boyfriend of yours? He's not too smart, leaving you alone."

"Snooty Hooty?" Elizabeth asked

"Yeah, that's Reece's name for Clara," said Matt as he loosened his grip and laughed. "Reece is a funny guy when he's not playing sheriff. He had a tough childhood so doesn't care much for the likes of Clara Richter. She's the one woman he and Griff have never had the same interest in which is odd because they usually compete for females. Reece thinks she looks like an owl with that little pinched nose and those big round eyes watching everybody. Would you like to meet her? She's a treat."

"Well, I don't think I'll care much for the likes of her either from the way you talk, but Margaret wants me to meet everyone."

"Good, just don't call her Snooty Hooty to her face."

Matt steered Elizabeth across the room to where Griffin and Clara were talking with Reece and Rachel. Elizabeth felt edgy the closer she got. The sheriff was correct. Those round eyes followed her every step without a change in expression. Elizabeth felt like she was an animal being inspected before a sale and soon led to slaughter. She was too self-conscious to speak by the time they reached the group.

"Clara, this is Elizabeth Rogers," said Griffin looking bored. "Moved into the Butcher place recently. She's from St. Louis originally."

"Yes, I know the Butcher place. You forget Griffin, my father owns the mill, so daddy sold them lumber. I'm surprised to see you received an invitation for this evening. The Spencers usually have an exclusive guest list. Of course, the Kellys and Richters have known the Spencers for years." She put her arm through Griff's and leaned in so close he took a step back. "Isn't that right, Griffin?"

"Will and Margaret invite all kinds of people to their home. Some they know because of business such as your father and some, like my family, are their friends. Besides, the Spencers knew Elizabeth's family back in St. Louis," answered Griff in a cynical tone.

Reece tittered and looked away with disdain. He expected nothing less of Clara. She was an obnoxious woman who clung to Griff because of money and prestige. Reece knew his friend had no true feelings for her. Clara was cold and manipulative and if the Kelly family was to suddenly suffer bad fortune, Clara wouldn't hesitate to release Griff from her clutches and move on to the next unfortunate man.

Despite pretenses, soft-hearted Griffin, who started and stopped relationships as frequently as Reece did, suffered remorse at breaking hearts. Griff was losing interest in Clara and her constant condescending attitude toward others. His break from her would be well received by the people closest to him.

Clara glared at Reece then turned an imitation smile toward Elizabeth. "So nice of Matt to help out a country girl."

Matt put his arm around Elizabeth and smiled broadly. "I agree Clara, I'm a lucky man. Elizabeth is a wonderful woman"

"Well if you excuse me," Rachel said with a deep sigh and her own artificial smile. "I hate to leave this interesting conversation, but I think I'll go rescue Bart from an engrossing discussion with his father about banking." She scurried across the room toward Mr. Ferguson and his son.

"I think it's time I get Elizabeth home also," said Matt. He shot his brother a look of disappointment wondering why he kept Clara around but vowed not to get involved. Griff had to come to that decision on his own and he hoped he did it soon. "I'll see you at home, Griff. We need to say goodbye to Will and Margaret."

"I think Margaret regrets not getting to spend more time with us this evening. I can tell she really likes you," said Matt on the way home. "She and my mother were close friends. She feels obligated to make sure we're all happy and that includes you. If you ever need advice she's a wise woman. Don't be afraid to ask for help."

"The only help I need is finding something to take to the garden club meeting in a few weeks. Despite my protest, it's the next event she's scheduled for me. Not that I mind really. I like the women I've met but it seems I'm always one step behind them. I had to scramble to think of something for the bazaar."

"The rock candy was a good idea," Matt interrupted. "Margaret loved it and so did the others."

"They're nice to me about everything so it's difficult to tell. I'm expected to take a plant to this meeting and once again, I have nothing. Henry built a flower box for the front porch and I haven't had time to look at it. I've been busy with the garden. Mrs. Ferguson did mention wild flowers that grow in the hills some place. White ones and purple. They're blooming now so they should be easy to dig up and transplant. I planned to take a ride up and see what I could find."

"No," Matt said firmly. "I don't want you anywhere near those hills. They're isolated and dangerous if you don't know where you're going. Reece says it's the first place men go when they're running from the law. I don't even like to go up there."

"You always act like I'm helpless. Must I remind you again that I have been on my own for some years now?"

"With your uncle's help."

"That's true but on my own none the less. I'm certain I can make a trip to these hills and back without any trouble."

Matt shook his head no for every argument Elizabeth made. Cougars roamed freely in those hills. He knew they fed off stray cattle from local ranches and it was foolish for her to go by herself. "Are you forgetting your encounter with the snake? I call that trouble. If you can't wade in a stream without recognizing danger, you have no business riding alone in the hills looking for flowers."

"Well then, I guess I can just stick a weed in a pot and haul that to the garden club meeting," Elizabeth said. "You have no idea how humiliating it will be without a decent flower." She was frustrated that Matt couldn't understand her point. Once again she felt as if no one had confidence in her to survive in this wild country."

"What if I found one of those flowers for you?" Matt said after a moment of silence between the two. I know the hills and I'm sure I can find something..."

Matt stopped mid-sentence with a look of shock at the crack of gunfire and a whizzing sound brushing past his face. A second shot sent his hat flying and he pushed Elizabeth to the floor of the buggy.

"Someone's shooting," he yelled. "Don't move."

He slapped the reins and shouted at the horses as they broke into a full run tossing the buggy from side to side as they galloped wildly down the road.

"Matt," Elizabeth screamed, trying to hold on. She was afraid she might bounce completely out.

"Stay down and hang on," Matt roared as he crouched as low as possible while trying to maintain control. "I'm going to try to get you home but if I'm hurt you'll have to take over. Do you think you can do that?"

"Matt, please," Elizabeth pleaded.

"Do you think you can do that?" Matt shouted.

"Yes, I'll do it. Just get us home."

The exhausted horses snorted as Matt pulled the buggy up to Elizabeth's house. He jumped down and pulled her out, pushing her toward the front door."

"Henry," she called, as she struggled to stay on the porch shouting until Luke burst from the bunk house with shotgun in hand. Henry followed behind, running barefoot across the yard.

"What the devil is going on?"

"Someone opened fire on us driving back. It was too dark to see who it was. She's fine but understandably shaken. Fortunately, the only thing hurt was my hat. It's back there on the road somewhere with a hole shot through it. Could just as well have been my head." Matt held Elizabeth who shook with fear as tears ran down her face.

"It was horrifying Henry. We could have been killed," cried Elizabeth. "Thank goodness Matt got us home safely. I was so scared." She buried her head in Matt's chest not wanting to think of what might have happened.

"You think it might have been the same guy that was sneaking around here last night?" Luke asked.

"I have no idea," answered Matt. "Nothing like this has ever happened. I can't imagine why someone would be shooting at us."

"I'm going to put a stop to this somehow. If Reece Cameron didn't take me serious before, he will now, or I'll take matters in my own hand." Henry was furious. There must be a way to track down the person responsible.

"Nothing we can do about it tonight, Henry," said Luke quietly. "It's too dark to go back to town now. We can't leave Miss Elizabeth alone and it's dangerous on that road if someone is shooting at people. We'll have to wait until morning."

"I know. We'd just be asking for more trouble," said Henry. "I hope Reece Cameron has a good night's rest because I'm not going to let him sleep a wink until he finds this man. You can bunk with us tonight Matt. I'll not have you trying to get home in the dark after this. Let's get your horses cooled down and in the barn. Elizabeth, get your things, you can sleep in the bunk house with us."

"No Henry, I'm sleeping in the house. I don't know who's trying to drive me from my home but it's going to take more than a few gunshots. The windows and door are locked, and I have a gun. I'll be perfectly safe and besides, if there's any trouble, you three are in the bunk house."

"Elizabeth, this is no time to argue," said Henry. He wasn't surprised that she repudiated his suggestion. He'd never seen a woman so determined to put herself in harm's way.

"I could stay in the house with her," said Matt. He glanced around at the startled faces of the other three and took a deep breath, clearing his throat before speaking again. "I mean, I could sleep downstairs and of course, Elizabeth would be upstairs in her bedroom." He paused again when he noticed Henry turn red and a slight grin appear on Luke's face. "With the door locked. Naturally, she would lock her bedroom door."

"That's a good idea," said Elizabeth, smiling at Matt. "That way I'm not alone and if there is any trouble then you could shoot anyone who tried to come in the house."

"I'll not have any of that sort of thing going on while I am ranch manager," Henry bellowed. "Why, I can just imagine the talk in town when this gets out. An unmarried woman entertaining a young man."

"I'm not entertaining anyone, Henry. I will be sound asleep in my bedroom with the locked door, remember? How dare you suggest anything else, if you believe that I'm that kind of woman, then the shame is on you, Henry Turner."

"I could sleep in the house if you want," said Luke, shyly raising his hand.

"No one is sleeping in the house," shouted Henry. "And that's final."

"Thank you, Luke," said Elizabeth, gritting her teeth. She narrowed her eyes and leered at Henry as she put her hands on her hips and stiffened her body, preparing for confrontation. "Matt volunteered to sleep in the house, downstairs. This is still my ranch and like it or not, I'm still in charge so there will be no discussion."

Elizabeth gathered her dress, turning sharply as she stomped into the house and slammed the door. Seconds later she meekly poked her head back out. "Could someone light the lamp for me?" she said with a sheepish look and timid voice. "I can't seem to find any matches."

The three men looked wide-eyed at each other waiting for someone to speak. Matt took another deep breath and looked down at the ground mumbling in a voice so low, Luke and Henry could barely hear. "When those blue eyes start glaring at you, there's no use in fighting. Take it from me, it's just best not to argue with her."

Henry and Luke both nodded in agreement and turned toward the bunk house in silence while Matt started up the porch steps. "I'd be glad to help, darlin'," he called out with a smile. "I believe I have a couple of matches right here in my pocket."

Elizabeth waited as Matt lit the lamp then led her upstairs, stopping at the bedroom door. "This is as far as I better go if I don't want Henry to storm in here with a shotgun."

"I know," Elizabeth whispered shyly. "I didn't mean to make such a fuss, but Henry treats me like a child."

"In a way, you are a child to him," Matt answered. "You're the same age as his daughter and when he looks at you he probably remembers his little girl. I don't think he intends to run your life, I think he's just trying to protect you like a father would protect his child."

Matt cupped Elizabeth's chin in his hand. "Even if she is a grown woman, who's been on her on for years and owns her own ranch, and doesn't need anyone else," he said mockingly.

"Stop making fun of me," Elizabeth laughed. "You just don't understand."

He moved his head close to hers, still holding her chin and kissed her lightly, lingering for a moment. "Then, teach me to understand," he whispered.

Elizabeth sighed and put her arms around his neck, kissing him again. "Matt," she said softly and nuzzled her face next to him, kissing his cheek.

"Elizabeth, are you up there?" Henry called from downstairs.

"Yes, Henry," Elizabeth gasped as she pushed Matt away. Fixing her hair, she walked to the top of the stairs. Henry has the worst timing, she thought.

"I just wanted to make sure you remembered to lock the door. Is Matt with you?"

She and Matt looked at each other knowing this was a planned entrance. Elizabeth gave him a little smile as she answered. "Yes Henry," sounding a little exasperated. "Matt was just walking me upstairs. He's coming down now."

Matt squeezed her hand as he descended the stairs to where Henry was standing. "I was making sure Elizabeth got to her room. I believe she's safely locked in,"

"Well then," Henry hesitated, glancing up at the top of the stairs and back at Matt. "I guess I'll go on out."

"No need to worry, Henry," said Matt looking toward the parlor. "I'll be uncomfortably sleeping down here, guarding the door. See you in the morning."

CHAPTER 11

A Job Well Done

Elizabeth found Luke sitting at the table when she walked into the kitchen. It was still early, and she was looking for Matt. She slept surprisingly well despite the events of the previous evening. She had lain in bed listening to the rain, thinking of the Spencer's party with satisfaction. It was good to see Jack Devlin once more and she had to admit she was surprised to find him still in town. She was even more surprised to find he'd lost his horse to Matt. Rachel was right. It's a sad situation for him to travel all this way only to end up losing the horse. Let that be a lesson to men and their silly card games, she thought as she stood looking out of the kitchen window toward the barn, hoping to see Matt and have a couple of moments alone before he left.

"He's already gone," Luke said casually as he drank his coffee. "He and Henry left at daybreak to see the sheriff." Luke pulled another chair back from the table and patted the seat. "Why don't you have some breakfast? Henry will fill you in when he gets back. Tell me about your party."

"He's already left? I didn't get a chance to say goodbye." Elizabeth sat down with a disappointed look on her face. She was hurt that Matt hadn't thought about her before going to town. It was true, they wanted to see Sheriff Cameron first thing and she'd slept longer than she should, but it couldn't be that big of a rush. After all, the shooting was over and that wouldn't change no matter how long they waited to tell Reece.

Luke walked to the stove and filled a plate with food, setting it in front of Elizabeth, watching her frown. He snickered to himself as he poured coffee into her cup. "Elizabeth?"

"Yes?" she said snapping out of her daydream.

"Matt drove the buggy home and got his horse. I guess he wanted to let Tom know about the shooting. He didn't want to wake you. Did you have a nice time at the party?"

"Yes, it was great fun. The Spencers must know everyone in town and I think they all showed up. Matt introduced me to Clara Richter who is a friend of his brother Griffin. I didn't really care for her. She made me feel like a country bumpkin completely out of place. Griffin is such a nice person and according to Matt, no one can understand why he bothers with her."

"I'm familiar with the Richter family and you wouldn't catch me within ten yards of them. I try to avoid Mr. Richter every time I go to the mill. His daughter is a pretty girl but getting mixed up with her is like falling into a rose briar patch. It's smells good, but those thorns are sharp and it sure is difficult to cut yourself free."

Elizabeth laughed at the comparison and wondered if Griff owned a sharp pair of pruning shears. "Oh, the gambler I met on the stage was there. It turns out he stayed in town and is doing some sort of business with Will Spencer. Rachel Kelly was swooning over him. It was quite comical. Matt, on the other hand, did not think any of it was too funny. I believe he's jealous."

"Seems like you and your cowboy are getting along better these days. Turns out he's not the man you thought he was," said Luke. "I've known his family for years. They're good people."

"I was wrong about him. Another lesson learned about not judging by first appearances."

"I think that goes for that gambler friend of yours," Luke said with a stern look. "Henry told me he was with you in town. Men like that can take advantage of young women and leave them high and dry. You're better off sticking with Matt Kelly and leaving the likes of that gambler alone."

"Why doesn't anyone like Jack?" Elizabeth asked. "He's been nothing but a gentleman to me and has never made a single inappropriate advance. Just because he's a gambler doesn't mean he's a bad person. I'm disappointed you feel that way, Luke."

"Disappointed or not," said Luke, still looking stern. "I know a thing or two and I stand by my opinion that you have no business with that fellow. Now, let's change the subject before we both get our dander up. Henry wanted me to remind you we were to clean out that brush today. It's starting to take over the fence and it'll pull it right over if we aren't careful. We'll have cattle spread out for miles if that happens. He said you two talked about it yesterday morning."

"I hate cleaning out brush," Elizabeth said "It's not fun."

"Well it's part of the job and needs to be done if you plan to run a ranch. Put on your overalls and take the wagon. The sickle and shovel are in the back. Take your gun with you in case you have trouble."

"Luke," Elizabeth hesitated. "Um, I don't technically know how to shoot."

"I thought you said last night you had a gun."

"Well I do have one, but it's an old one of my late husband's and although I've shot a rifle, I never hit much. I don't know how to use the pistol."

Luke groaned and shook his head heaving an exasperated sigh. "Well then, if you see someone who looks like trouble, shoot in the air and I'll come running. If that doesn't startle them then shoot over their head. That'll probably scare them off." He smiled teasingly. "Try not to hit them. They may be a neighbor."

"Or a snake of the human variety," said Elizabeth. "Aren't you going too?"

"I'll catch up later. I want to go out to that far pasture to check on the herd. There was lightning last night with that storm and I want to make sure we didn't lose any steer."

Elizabeth rummaged through a drawer and found the gun then went upstairs to change while Luke hitched up the wagon. Luke advised her to cut across the pasture because of the rain-soaked roads and she rambled toward the fence. She was to cut the brush and vines as far back as possible and throw everything into a pile. Luke suspected it would be too wet to burn and that job would have to wait for later in the afternoon or another day.

The brush was thick with wild grape vines wound tightly around the fence. Elizabeth moaned as she thought of cutting and pulling them off. Huckleberry and Gooseberry were growing along the road threatening to overtake the path. Other bushes were mixed in. She was thankful Luke had given her a pair of leather work gloves although they were too big, and she made a mental note to buy some at the feed and supply the next time she was in town.

Hours passed, and the work was slow. The sun came out and humidity was high. She brushed her hair from her face as the frizzy strands fell over her eyes. Why hadn't she thought of wearing her sun hat? Luke was right. One section of the fence was starting to lean and in need of replacing. Once the Huckleberry was cut and piled away from the road, she started on the bushes.

A large green plant loomed in the way and Elizabeth wished she'd brought an axe but didn't want to take the time to go all the way back to the barn. She wasn't sure the sickle would do the job. The next time this chore needed taken care of, she was trading jobs with Luke and she would check on cattle while he chopped away at the bushes. The large green monster was particularly troublesome, and she knelt on hands and knees, crawling underneath to survey what she needed to take it down and figuring it may have to wait for an axe after all.

"May I be of service?" a voice behind her asked. Elizabeth backed out and peered through the gap between her side and bent arm as an upside-down Jack Devlin stood staring with great interest at her bent over behind sticking up in the air.

She got to her feet as gracefully as possible and faced him, blushing. "Jack, what are you doing here," she stuttered with embarrassment. "How did you find me?"

"No one was home and I noticed the fresh wheel tracks through your pasture, so I took a chance you might be at the point where they stopped. Looks like I was correct."

His eyes moved up and down, still smiling wryly as he admired her dressed in pants and man's shirt. "Again, I commend you on your courage in becoming a woman rancher. I hadn't realized it would entail such grueling work. I came for the lunch you owe me but instead am prepared to assist you in this task."

Jack walked to the wagon taking off his jacket and threw it on the seat, rolled up his sleeves and walked back. "Where should I begin?"

"Jack, you can't clear brush wearing your suit. It'll be ruined." Elizabeth looked at his grey suit pants with perfect crease and white silk shirt. He was certainly a well-dressed man. How many suits did he carry with him, she wondered?

"Nonsense Mrs. Rogers, I always do dirty, physical work dressed like this. Actually, I believe it's been many years and I never was much for getting my hands dirty but if you let me help, I will do my best. My father owned an export business in New Orleans and I spent most of my time behind a desk or down at the docks watching bales of cotton loaded onto ships." He bent over and raised the bottom branches, kicking at the dirt surrounding the root system.

"I didn't realize, Jack. I figured you for a southerner. I'm afraid your accent gave you away on that one and of course you told me you traveled, but I'm curious about how you moved from an export business in Louisiana to a gambler in San Francisco or Denver or where ever you call home."

"It's simple," said Jack over his shoulder as he walked to the wagon and pulled out the shovel. "War."

"Yes," said Elizabeth, her voice dropping to a murmur. "The war of the rebellion. It affected everyone I'm afraid. I don't think I told you I lost my brother at Shiloh." She looked at Jack with tears welling in her eyes and continued. "Alex made it through only to come home with haunting memories. He drowned less than a mile from our house. I know all about that war."

"We preferred to call it our war for independence, our fight for the cause." Jack dug the shovel into the ground, breaking through the surface and pulled out a chunk of dirt which he threw to the side. He raised his head with a forlorn face. "We were foolish to think the Yankees would let us go. Did your brother fight for the north or the glorious Confederacy?"

"Union infantry under General Grant," Elizabeth said. "Alex served under Dodge, Sixteenth Corps."

Jack began to dig again continually throwing shovels of dirt with increasing velocity. "My brother died at Chancellorsville. He was seventeen. I was beside him when he fell. Like your husband, I made it home uninjured but with scars all the same. My family's business was in ruins and my mother mad with grief." He threw the shovel to the side and bent down to wrestle with a stubborn root. "I stayed in New Orleans for a couple of years until the cotton business was revived and we could resume our export business, but it wasn't the same." Tearing the root from the ground he threw it to the side and stood, facing Elizabeth.

"I think I saw a rope in the wagon." Jack walked to the wagon and shifted the tools around. Pulling out a sturdy rope, he tied it to the undercarriage and returned, kneeled on the ground and tied the rope around the strongest part of the root system.

"In my father's eyes, my brother's death was somehow my fault and our relationship worsened over time," he continued. "I spent my youth watching riverboats travel the Mississippi and one day I climbed aboard one, leaving my parents and three sisters behind. I got a job running the roulette table aboard the Orleans Belle then started playing cards. Once I was good enough, I came west with a lot of other ex-confederates, bought a share in the White Swan gambling house and made my fortune."

He climbed on the seat of the wagon and took the reins. "If you'll stand back, Mrs. Rogers, I'm going to attempt to pull the stump out." Slapping the reins, the horses moved forward slowly as the thick root gave way and tore from the ground. "There, that ought to do it."

"I'm sorry Jack. We all carry sorrows from the past long after they should have been forgotten. War is a terrible thing that leaves our lives in shambles." She looked at the large bundle of roots with the rope still wound around them. "I couldn't have done this without you. It does seem that I owe you lunch and if you follow me back to the house I'll be glad to fix something although not the quality you would get at the hotel."

"I'm sure it will be as charming as its host. Lead the way, Mrs. Rogers."

"Any man who pulls a clump of roots like that out of the ground can call me Elizabeth. Follow me, Mr. Devlin."

Once back at the house, Elizabeth showed Jack into a small wash room by the kitchen while she ran upstairs to change. She scrunched her face in horror when she saw her frizzy curls scattered about her head and quickly ran a brush through which only served to create more frizz. Finally, she wet a comb and moistened her hair, pulling it tight into a roll on top of her head and adding a ribbon for decoration. Throwing on a clean dress she returned to the kitchen to find Jack waiting.

"I'm afraid leftover stew is on the menu for today. It won't take a moment to heat up," said Elizabeth. "I don't live a fancy life on the ranch. Not like you do in your travels."

"Ah, but what a fine life it must be for you. Working your land, raising cattle, sleeping in the same bed every night. It's a life of peace and comfort, I'm sure," said Jack.

"So far, the only land I've worked is my garden," laughed Elizabeth. "And I haven't had the chance to raise my cattle although Henry is softening to the idea of letting me go on the cattle drive. Sleeping in the same bed every night is very comforting and sitting on the porch in the evening is the most peaceful part of my day. Except for the last couple of nights. Things have been anything but peaceful. "

"How's that?" asked Jack as he watched Elizabeth standing at the stove stirring the pot.

"It started the night of the church bazaar. There was a prowler sneaking around outside the house. I saw him from my bedroom window, all dressed in black and looking up at me. It was quite frightening to say the least." Elizabeth ladled the stew onto Jack's plate as he cut a piece of bread. "Do you prefer tea or coffee?"

"Tea with a bit of milk if you have it," answered Jack. "A prowler? What do you think he was looking for?"

"No one knows. Henry thinks he's interested in me since he was spotted by the window before running through the dark to the road with Luke and his shotgun hot on the trail. I must admit I was sitting by the window enjoying the cool evening and hadn't drawn the curtains." Elizabeth set the tea cup in front of Jack and sat down looking contrite. I'm afraid I was only partially dressed as I sat in my rocker. It was all very humiliating."

"What did our Sheriff Cameron say about this? Who does he feel is responsible?"

"Who knows," shrugged Elizabeth. "Reece thought it somewhat humorous I was seen sitting in my own home in my petticoat." She gasped as she put her hand over her mouth, looking at Jack with big eyes. "I'm sorry, I shouldn't have said that. It isn't appropriate for us to speak of those things."

Jack laughed out loud and placed his hand on her shoulder. "My dear Elizabeth, we're both adults. Certainly, you realize I understand a little about what a woman wears under her skirts. Now tell me, could you recognize this man? You said he was dressed in black."

"No, it was too dark and neither Henry nor Luke could see any more than a shadow running from the back of the house. It was frightening. But the worse thing was last night coming home from the Spencer's party. Someone started shooting at us."

"What do you mean shooting at you?" said Jack with a curious look.

"Matt and I were enjoying the evening ride home from the party when someone opened fire on us. Shot Matt's hat off. He's lucky he wasn't killed. We're both lucky we weren't killed by bullets or broken neck when thrown from the racing buggy. Elizabeth shot a frightened look at Jack. "It was downright scary. Henry felt it best that Matt stay here for the night and they left early this morning to talk with Sheriff Cameron."

"I'm sorry your life was in danger. What do you suspect is the reason for all of this?" asked Jack.

"I can't think of a reason why someone would want to kill us, but Luke sent me out this morning with an old pistol for protection just the same. I don't even know how to shoot."

"I would be happy to assist you with that as well," said Jack. He took his watch from his pocket and checked the time. "I can stay for a while to show you a few things before I leave. I have an appointment later in the day."

"What a beautiful pocket watch. Such an intricate design on the front," said Elizabeth taking it from Jack.

"It belonged to my grandfather. A grand gentleman who was very dear to me. The woman's picture inside is my grandmother. They were married fifty years and I never saw a happier couple. Of course, they've both been gone for many years but I think of them almost daily. That watch is one of the few things I took with me when I left home. It is my most valuable possession."

"How wonderful," said Elizabeth. "I have some things from my family as well. My mother's china and a few silver pieces. My father's family bible and a box filled with wooden soldiers and other trinkets belonging to Jim. Alex didn't own much when we met but I do have the old gun and pictures. Like you, they are worth more than gold to me."

"How about those shooting lessons now? We still have some time," said Jack. "I have my pistol with me and a rifle on my horse. Which would you prefer?"

Elizabeth hesitated for a moment. "I think I better try the pistol since that's my only weapon." She laid the watch on the table and walked to the window. "There are some old bottles in the barn. We could use them for targets, I guess."

"I believe those will work," smiled Jack as he headed for the door. "Let's go give it a try."

They dug out all the bottles they could find in the barn and placed them on top of the corral fence closest the pasture. Jack loaded his pistol and passed it to Elizabeth who aimed and fired. The crack of the gun cut through the air but not a thing moved on top of the fence.

"I think I missed," said Elizabeth with a nervous laugh. She was surprised at the recoil of the gun as her arm jerked back.

"It takes a time or two," Jack said with a laugh. He put his arms around her and steadied the gun as she held it. "Try it again," he said softly in her ear.

Elizabeth squeezed the trigger slowly. Not a single bottle moved, and she looked at Jack with disappointment.

"That was better. You'll get use to it," he said. He put his arm around her again, moving his cheek next to hers and adjusted the gun slightly upward. "One more time, just a little higher."

The bullet whizzed past the bottle and knocked it to the ground although it was not hit with a bullet and Elizabeth jumped excitedly. Jack laughed out loud as he watched. "Kudos Elizabeth. You're quickly becoming a sharpshooter."

"But I haven't hit anything yet," Elizabeth said.

Thirty minutes later a bullet ripped through a bottle, shattering it as it flew off the fence. Jack smiled with pride as he held up a broken piece for inspection. Bottles continued to fall with subsequent shots and by the end of practice, Elizabeth's hand ached from holding the gun.

"I leave you a seasoned marksman, Elizabeth," said Jack as they walked toward the house. "As much as I would like to stay and continue your training, I'm afraid I must be going. Promise me that you'll keep yourself out of danger and if the shooting starts again, stay away from the open windows."

"I thought you said I was a seasoned marksman?" said Elizabeth. "I can defend myself now."

Jack grabbed Elizabeth's arm and came to a stop, scowling as he spoke. "It's a dangerous world Elizabeth and a man will stop at nothing to get what he wants. Take care you don't get in the way." He released her and stared as she rubbed her arm where he had held it.

"I'll remember," she said faintly.

His face brightened again, and he kissed her hand. "I thank you for the lovely lunch and entertainment, but this still won't get you out of joining me for dinner at the hotel before I leave."

"I'll see what I can do," answered Elizabeth with an uneasy look. She stood on the porch watching Jack mount his horse and waved as he rode off, thinking about Jack's comments and what Luke said at breakfast then walked into the house groaning about returning to her work and the piles of brush she left by the fence.

CHAPTER 12

THE WAGON ON MILL ROAD

What was Jack Devlin talking about, wondered Elizabeth as she walked into the kitchen. Despite the hard work of clearing brush, including digging out an extremely stubborn green monstrosity, they spent an enjoyable morning together and she thought they were becoming good friends after sharing stories of their past. Jack's warning about getting in the way was alarming. Why did she need to be cautioned? She shrugged her shoulders deciding it was nothing important involving her and turned her attention to finishing the job of clearing brush when she caught sight of Jack's watch sitting on the table. She remembered laying it down and he must have forgotten to pick it up. Poor Jack, thought Elizabeth. That watch means so much to him and he'd be worried sick to think it was lost. She needed to return it as soon as possible and if she hurried, she could catch up with him on the road.

Elizabeth ran to the buckboard still loaded with tools thinking Jack wouldn't be far ahead and traveled about a mile before realizing she'd never actually gone to town by herself. Henry always took her, and she usually spent most of the time talking instead of paying attention to which direction they headed. This now posed a problem. It's amazing, she thought, how she hadn't noticed before that the scenery was undistinguishable and she slowed at a crossroad to study her surroundings and faced the dilemma of choosing to take a gently curving path to the left or sharper turn to the right. Neither looked familiar so Elizabeth opted for a path closest to a clump of trees remembering she passed a clump of trees on a previous trip to town. She maneuvered the wagon around the corner looking behind her at the other road. There were no fresh tracks going in either direction which was curious. No matter which path Jack took, he should have left some sign that he had passed through. The wagon rumbled slowly as she carefully drove the team along the next part of the road which turned substantially muddier the farther she went. The overnight rain left pools of water-filled ruts and old wheel tracks which filled the road with deep impressions.

"See Elizabeth, all you need is a little confidence," she said, talking to herself and urging the horses along. "You don't need help from any of those men. You can cut down bushes, plant a garden and drive a wagon through mud, despite what they may think."

The farther she went the worse the road became. The ruts were difficult to navigate as the horses strained to pull the wagon which was sinking with every inch they moved. Elizabeth stopped and looked around listening for a sign of other people on the road. It was odd she hadn't met anyone else along the way by now. In fact, the only sign of life was a bee who insisted on buzzing around her face. She swatted the air and looked back at the road, wondering if it was wise to go on. At this rate, it would take the rest of the day to get to town and Jack was too far ahead to catch. She hadn't left a note for Luke and considering the events of the last couple of nights he might be concerned if he found her gone. The only choice was to turn back. She took a deep breath and angled the wagon around for the turn, coming to an abrupt stop when the left front wheel sank deep into a large mud hole making it impossible for the horses to move. "What now?" Elizabeth mumbled. She jumped down and grabbed the bridle of a horse trying to lead them along, sinking up to her ankles.

"Should have changed back into those pants," said Elizabeth, looking at the horse who snorted and turned his head away as if to show his disgust at their current situation. "Why didn't you tell me the roads were this bad? You and I have spent the entire day together and this is the way it ends." She pulled the skirt of her dress up and tucked it in her waist to keep some of the mud off and yanked the horses forward again, but the wagon was buried too deep as it sat cross ways in the road

Exasperated, Elizabeth looked for a tree branch to use as leverage. She needed one that was good-sized but anything she found that was suitable was too large for her to drag to the wagon. Waving her hand around her face at the persistent bee, she found one that was a manageable size and pulled it to the road where she strained to lift it up far enough to cram it under the wheel. Leaning with all her weight on the limb, Elizabeth could not get the wheel to budge. Next, she tried jumping up and down, pushing with all her power until it cracked in two, sending her face first into the mud.

She lay there momentarily, exhausted and with no idea what to do next. Tears welled in her eyes as she stood, wiping mud from her mouth. "How are we going to explain this?" she said to the horse that stood motionless as she rubbed his face, and sniffled. "What do you think I should do? I can leave you here with the wagon and walk back by myself but what if someone comes along and steals you? Maybe I could leave the wagon and take you back with me." She closed her eyes and leaned her head against the horse. "Why is everything so difficult?"

"Where were you planning to go in that wagon?"

Elizabeth lifted her head but didn't turn around. She felt relieved to hear Matt's voice and wanted to run and jump into his arms but instead rubbed the horse's neck while she formulated her story.

Matt climbed down from his horse and walked to Elizabeth, wrapping his arms around her and drawing her close.

"How did you find me?" she said, not wanting to make eye contact.

"It wasn't difficult. Henry and I got back to the ranch after talking to Reece and found Luke frantic. The wagon was gone, and I guess he imagined the worst. We knew you weren't on the road to town because we just came from that direction..."

"But I'm on the road to town," Elizabeth interrupted.

"No, you're on the road to the mill," Matt said. "The ruts are deep in this road because they haul wagons full of trees ready to be cut into lumber. They're heavy and make deep tracks. That rain last night made this road impassable. No one would try to make it through the mud down here today, except you and whoever was following behind. And me, of course, when I realized you went this way."

"What do you mean the person behind me? I haven't seen or heard a thing except a bee that refuses to leave me alone. In fact, it's been eerily quiet." Elizabeth turned to face Matt. "Do you think it was Jack?"

Matt followed the bee with his eyes as it lit on Elisabeth's hair. Reaching out with a swiping motion, he grabbed the insect, squeezing it in his hand, and then let it drop to the ground. "That's one problem solved."

"I've got two questions," Matt went on. "First, why the heck would Jack Devlin be out here following you and second, why didn't he bother to help? I picked up those tracks back by the turn of the road. They came out of nowhere, probably from the brush and then headed this way. They turned off the road a little way back and disappeared into the grass again. If he's such a gentleman, why did he leave you stranded out here? He must have known you'd be in trouble the further you went."

"Maybe he realized he left his pocket watch at my ranch and was trying to find me. Still, that doesn't explain why he would not call out to me or try to catch up." Elizabeth had a puzzled look on her face remembering the way Jack acted before he left.

"He left his watch at your ranch? When was he there and why?"

A guilty look came over Elizabeth's face as she thought about the morning she spent with Jack and how Matt would react. She cringed to think of how she would explain Jack's visit. "I didn't ask him to come. He showed up this morning and helped me take out a huge bush which was really more like a tree. Then during lunch, he showed me his grandfather's pocket watch and taught me to shoot."

"He was the one doing the shooting? Luke went wild when he heard gunfire. He was sure you were in danger."

"I didn't think," Elizabeth said as her voice cracked. "I told Jack about someone shooting at us last night and he offered to teach me to use that old pistol." She smiled sheepishly at Matt and kissed his cheek lightly. "If it makes you feel better, he didn't do a very good job. I still can't hit a thing."

"It doesn't make me feel better at all. In fact, it makes me angry. He's trouble Elizabeth and I would prefer you stayed away from him." Matt noticed a beam of light dancing on the wheel of the wagon and pulled Elizabeth closer as he looked around.

"What's wrong?" asked Elizabeth tensely as she watched Matt's face.

"Maybe nothing. I just saw a flicker of light move over the wagon. It reminded me of something that happens when sunlight reflects off a mirror. If I didn't know better, I'd say someone was using it as a signal."

Elizabeth looked in the direction Matt spoke of and thought she saw a glimmer of moving light. "Who do you think it is?"

"I'm not sure. I don't know who made those tracks in the mud and don't like the fact that they disappeared as quickly as they appeared. Henry and I will worry about the wagon later."

He unhitched Elizabeth's horse and led the animal to the grass on the side of the road. Helping Elizabeth onto the saddle, he looked around once more and touched the gun in his holster. "We'll stay off to the side and out of the mud until we get to the main road. This could be a dangerous situation and if any trouble starts I want you to stay out of the way. You ride that horse as fast as you can and don't stop until you get home."

"That's what Jack said," Elizabeth mumbled. "It's a dangerous world, stay out of the way."

"What did you say?"

"Nothing," Elizabeth answered. She was afraid to tell Matt about the conversation she had with Jack earlier. A conversation that hadn't frightened her before but made her leery now. She suspected he was up to something but uncertain what it might be.

"What did Reece say about the shooting last night?" Elizabeth asked, curious about the sheriff's take on all that happened.

"He doesn't think it's a coincidence that all this has started since Jack Devlin arrived in town. I've about got him convinced Devlin is behind all of it. Reece wants to know more about him and this gambling house he owns. If your gambler friend is involved in anything illegal, Reece will find it. The sheriff is a difficult man to reckon with if you're the one breaking the law."

"Why would Jack shoot at us? What would be the point?" Elizabeth questioned Matt's theory and passed it off as jealousy.

He wasn't thinking clearly and too easily ready to blame Jack. She couldn't believe her friend would hurt her. "You can say the same thing about me. Jack and I arrived at the same time."

"That's quite a feat for you to lay in wait for yourself as we rode home. What magician's trick did you use for that one? How about the man outside your window? Was that you also?"

"Don't be absurd, of course I didn't do those things, but it doesn't mean Jack was responsible either. I find that just as unlikely." Elizabeth stared at Matt in disgust.

"Isn't it interesting that your friend Mr. Devlin is never around when the trouble starts? He miraculously had an excuse on each occasion. If you remember he left the Spencer's party early last night because of a late appointment. He knew I was bringing you home and it sure would be easy to wait unseen somewhere for us to drive by."

"I don't believe it and won't listen to another word." Elizabeth grew quiet as they rode along. She followed Matt's gaze as he looked from side to side and behind, keeping watch for anything out of the ordinary.

"Was Henry mad?" she said, finally breaking the silence and trying to change the subject. "About me leaving without saying something to Luke."

"Not mad, just worried," replied Matt. "When Luke heard the gun shots he hightailed it to the fence where you were supposed to be working. When you weren't there he went back to the house, panicked at what he might find. He saw two plates from your lunch with Devlin." Matt shot a disapproving look at Elizabeth. "Real friendly of you to fix him a meal," he said sarcastically.

"What was I to do? He really was a big help to me and I felt obliged to offer something." She looked away again and was quiet, not wishing to talk about Jack Devlin and after a time tried once more to change the subject.

"Matt, did you know Henry's family when they lived here? Do you remember his daughters?"

"I knew Pearl, the oldest. She would have been eight or nine when her mother took her back east. I remember my parents talking about it and how crushed Henry was. The younger one, Mae, was Rachel's age. Maybe three. Why?"

"Just curious," answered Elizabeth. "Luke said Henry's wife moved back to Kansas and he lost touch with them. It's a wonder it didn't destroy him completely. Where in Kansas did they move, I wonder?"

"Lawrence, I think. Henry saw wagon trains leaving almost daily and decided to come west too. My pa could never understand why his wife would take their children back. I'm not meaning to change the subject, but I forgot to tell you we saw Dutch Jordan in town. Reece and I paid a little visit to see how well he really knows Devlin. He sold Jack the thoroughbred and set up our poker game. I don't think Reece has ever trusted Dutch. He's checking him out too."

"What did Dutch say about Jack?"

"Not much, that's why Reece is suspicious. Dutch was pretty vague about details but said they have a mutual business acquaintance."

"I suppose the sheriff is checking him out too?"

"Yes Ma'am, he sure is," laughed Matt. "That's what makes Reece good at his job. The reason I mention Dutch is because he wants me to enter my horse in a race sponsored by the Elkhorn Saloon. They have one every year so those of us who like to brag about our ability to judge good horse flesh can put our money where our mouth is. I've never entered but that thoroughbred is the finest horse I've ever seen, and I just may have to race him."

"Your horse? You mean Jack's horse."

"I won him fair and square so he's mine now which is why Jack Devlin doesn't like me. Dutch says Devlin wants to set up another poker game. He's determined to get the horse back one way or the other and wants me to name the place and time. That's why Reece and I believe Jack is the one who's behind this shooting. Revenge for beating him at his own game."

Matt tipped his hat slightly and smiled at Elizabeth. "That and the fact that I'm the one escorting you around instead of him. With all that's gone on I haven't had a chance to show the horse off. I thought I might take you over to the Emerald tomorrow and give you a chance to ride him."

"I'm not sure how Henry will feel about me leaving the ranch, but I'd love to see this coveted animal everyone is talking about," Elizabeth laughed.

"You'll be fine with me," Matt said. "Speaking of Henry, he picked up a letter for you when we were in town. It's from your uncle."

"Ugh," groaned Elizabeth. "I hope Will Spencer didn't send word about this trouble. My uncle will want me to go back to St. Louis now, for sure." She straightened in the saddle and looked stubbornly at Matt. "I'm not going, no matter what he says. Henry thinks we ought to get a good price for the cattle, so the ranch will pay for itself and I can pay my uncle back for helping me get started."

"Don't take it out on me," grinned Matt. "I don't want you to go anywhere. If you need money to keep your ranch operating and your uncle isn't willing to help anymore, then I will. I'll give you anything you want."

Elizabeth didn't answer but her flushed color and smiling eyes were all Matt needed. He was surprised to hear himself make this offer to a woman he barely knew, but there was something about her that made him want to hold on and he was willing to fight Jack Devlin or anyone else to keep her.

"My uncle is a good man and I've done him a disservice to speak badly of him. This is my home now and nothing is going to change that."

CHAPTER 13

NUTTAH

Matt opened the barn door and led Elizabeth inside. The smell of fresh straw permeated the air as they walked passed each stall to where a buckskin horse stood majestically waiting. Elizabeth reached out to scratch the white star on his forehead.

"I can see why everyone wants to own him," Elizabeth said. "He's beautiful. What do you call this fine fellow?"

"Well, it's an interesting story," laughed Matt, watching the reaction of the horse to Elizabeth's touch. "The original Texas owner called him Napayshini which is Sioux for courageous and strong. I was thinking of calling him Nuttah meaning my heart until Griff put an end to that idea. It seems he thought that name was not deserving of a steed like this. A little too mushy for his taste. He felt a horse of this stature needed a more gallant name so I'm just calling him Buck."

"Oh, I agree," laughed Elizabeth, sarcastically. "Buck is a much more gallant name. My Heart doesn't seem appropriate. What made you think of that one?"

Matt smiled as he pulled a playing card from his pocket, handing it to Elizabeth. "This too is an interesting story. The night I played poker with Devlin, I was holding five of the worst cards I've ever seen. I was sure I would lose the hand, my money, and my horse. This queen of hearts was part of that hand and I had to discard her in hopes of picking up a seven which is exactly what happened. I couldn't have planned it better."

Elizabeth stroked the face of the card gently as if it were a precious possession. "I don't understand. If the card was so important why did you get rid of it?

Matt nodded his head in agreement, embarrassed at Elizabeth's question. "I know it's silly but as soon as I saw the hand I was sure this queen of hearts would be lucky for me. Call it superstition if you will, but she got me the seven I needed to win, so after the game I kept the card and she's been lucky for me ever since. I found you, didn't I?"

"We found each other." Elizabeth blushed as she handed the card back. She was touched by the story and Matt's sentiment. He wasn't the only lucky one and once again she remembered their first meeting and the disaster that turned into something so sweet. "I have to admit I agree with Griffin but if it's any consolation, I like the name Buck."

Matt chuckled again. "You side with my brother and not me? I'll remember that. I wish he would keep that barn door latched. I found it open this morning. If this horse gets out of his stall, I'm afraid he might be long gone. I wonder where Griff's head is sometimes. Let me saddle him so you can take a ride. We'll go down by that stream again. I promise I'll warn you this time if I shoot a snake."

"That's comforting, but I'm hoping we don't run into any."

Matt threw the saddle on Buck and handed the reins to Elizabeth. "He's yours for the taking. At least temporarily. You can run him for a little when we get out in the open. It's good warm up for the race."

"So, you've decided to enter? I was hoping you would. It seems like a shame to have a thoroughbred such as him if you're not going to race him." Elizabeth petted Buck's neck and ran her fingers through his thick mane. "I'm excited to watch. Do you think people will place bets?"

"As a matter of fact, I do," said Matt. "Cowboys love to brag about who has the fastest horse. Men spend all evening at the Elkhorn telling stories of their horse's strength and endurance. The more whiskey a man drinks, the better the stories get. My father always talks about a Sorrel horse he had years ago before Rachel and Lance were born. Seems this horse out ran a pack of Indians near the Snake River while hunting. Griff and I aren't sure that story is true, but Pa has quite a talent for telling a good yarn. I guarantee nobody's seen a horse like Buck. He's been the topic of conversation since the card game and as soon as Griff finds out I'm going to race, he'll take bets from every man in town. Save your money darlin' because you can win enough to pay off what you owe on your ranch if you get lucky."

"Hang on to that queen of hearts," Elizabeth grinned. "It sounds like she's the only luck we'll need." Elizabeth slapped the reins on the side of the horse and dug her feet tight into the stirrup. "Come on Buck. Let's see what you can do."

Buck put his head down and galloped through the field with Elizabeth practically lying on his back, leaving Matt behind. The horse dug his hooves deep into the grass, snorting with hot breath as his smooth stride moved them along. Elizabeth looked over her shoulder and saw Matt crossing the field on his horse and laughed as Buck inched ahead further. She finally slowed to let Matt catch up, praising the thoroughbred softly as he trotted along.

"He's quite a horse," she called out.

"You're quite a jockey. I may have to let you race him," grinned Matt. "Where did you learn to ride like that?"

"My brother Jim taught me. We used to race, but it wasn't the same on our plow horses. It's one of my favorite memories. I didn't tell you that the letter I got from my uncle was good news. Apparently Will has been sending him updates about the ranch and reported that I was doing a good job. I think Henry had something to do with it too. Will told my uncle that I, along with my ranch, are becoming self-sufficient which must have impressed my uncle because he didn't mention a thing about going home."

"That's nice because I didn't want to have to send your uncle a message that I wasn't going to let you leave Nevada. I think you should invite your uncle for a visit, so he can see for himself how things are going," said Matt, reaching out for Elizabeth's hand. "I'd like to meet him and hope he and I will be friends."

Elizabeth smiled shyly. It was surreal that she should find herself this happy with a man such as Matt. She had no intentions of ever falling in love when she boarded the train in St. Louis and she realized now, it was quickly becoming a reality. Her uncle would like Matt, she was sure.

"Perhaps you can meet him some day," she said. "Will has encouraged him to come for a visit. Those two haven't seen each other for years and it would do my uncle good to get away from his work. I don't know if his wife and children would be willing to come along and I must admit I don't know where I would put all six of them if they did. It would be quite a challenge, that's for sure."

"They can stay at the Emerald. We have plenty of room and I'm sure Pa and your uncle would get along."

"It would be nice to see them," said Elizabeth. "I admit I've been a little home sick. I may mention that in my next letter." She glanced at Matt mischievously. "Come on, I'll race you back."

Griffin was in the barn when the two returned and took the horse's reins as Elizabeth dismounted. "You should feel privileged Elizabeth. He hasn't let me ride Buck yet. If I didn't know better, I'd say he liked you more than me."

"A blind man could see that," said Matt sarcastically. "You don't think I'm going to let you anywhere near that horse after you left the barn door unhitched this morning? You're lucky Elizabeth and I came out here early. You'd never hear the end of it from Pa if any of these horses got out and I don't have the time to run them down. Neither do you for that matter."

"I hope you're kidding with that comment because this is the first time I've been out here all day so don't start accusing me. Maybe Rach left it open."

"She wasn't up when Elizabeth got here," said Matt inspecting the tack room. "Is anything missing?"

"I haven't paid attention," said Griff, following behind. "Do you think someone's been in here that shouldn't be?"

"I don't have a good feeling about this." Matt glanced at Elizabeth who was brushing Buck. Careful what you say around her. She's convinced Devlin is innocent of any wrong doing and it won't help to mention his name in connection with any of this."

"You think Devlin's been sneaking around here?" Griffin whispered. "Reece stopped by after you left. He's got some new information about Elizabeth's favorite gambler."

Matt scowled at his brother and took a deep breath, gnashing his teeth. "I'd appreciate it if you didn't put it that way. Not if you want to stay on my good side. Is Rachel in the house?"

"Yeah," said Griffin nodding as he turned to speak to Elizabeth. "Rachel was asking about you earlier. She hasn't seen you since the Spencer party. Why don't you go on in and see if you can find her while Matt and I finish up here? We'll catch up as soon as we're done."

They watched as Elizabeth walked toward the house, brushing the horses and waiting until she opened the door before Griff spoke again.

"Jack Devlin is broke."

"What?" Matt said in astonishment.

"Dead broke according to Reece." Griff threw up his hands in amazement and chuckled. "Mr. Fancy Pants is in debt up to his mustache. Owes money to just about everyone and some of them aren't nice. Remember the game in Denver before he took the stage here? He was not a big winner and in fact, came away empty handed."

"No wonder Buck means so much to him. He told us he could make a bundle racing," said Matt. "I understand now why he dislikes me so much. So, what's Reece going to do about it?

"Nothing," answered Griffin. "Devlin hasn't broken the law and isn't wanted for a crime anywhere as far as Reece can tell."

"Look at all the things that have happened. The man sneaking around Elizabeth's ranch, someone shooting as us. I'm positive there was someone on the mill road yesterday when I found Elizabeth in the wagon. If he hurts her, Reece will have to arrest me."

"How do you know Devlin wants to hurt Elizabeth?" Griff raised his eyebrows in a skeptical look. "She's not the one who took his horse. Do me a favor and let Reece take care of this and don't do anything stupid."

"I've got this feeling in my gut that I can't get rid of," said Matt. "If it's just me against Devlin then I can handle him, but Elizabeth is wrapped up in the middle of it all and I'm not sure how to keep her out."

"Give her a little credit for being smart enough to realize that after being shot at while bouncing around on the floor of a buggy, there's a possibility that she might be in a little danger. Even if her judgment about Jack Devlin isn't the best, if you ask her to keep her distance, she'll listen to you."

Matt looked doubtful as he threw the brush down and led Buck into his stall. He wasn't sure Elizabeth would listen to him when it came to Devlin. Jack was, after all, her favorite gambler. Still, she needed to take precautions.

"Come on Matt, stop worrying about Mr. Fancy Pants. You know Elizabeth doesn't care about him, although I must say, he's the slickest dresser I've ever come across." Griffin chuckled as he looked toward the house. "Maybe you should get one of those silk shirts with the ruffles. It's guaranteed to make you popular with the ladies." He winked at Matt who leered back and heaved a disgusted sigh.

"I'm worried about Elizabeth, not Devlin."

"Then I suggest you talk to Henry," said Griff. "He doesn't like the guy anymore than the rest of us. I'm sure he and Luke will do what they can to keep Elizabeth as far away from Jack Devlin as possible. Besides, Devlin can't stay around here forever waiting to win his horse back. He's a smart gambler and will have to cut his losses and move on. It's a matter of time."

CHAPTER 14

A RIDE TO REMEMBER

E lizabeth was giddy with excitement on the day of the race. Once the news got out that Matt had entered his thoroughbred, the entire town was talking and, as Matt predicted, Griffin spent most of his free time collecting bets from men at the Elkhorn Saloon or anyone else for that matter. Elizabeth put five dollars on Buck despite Henry's disapproval. He thought it improper for a lady to engage in horse betting and gave her the traditional parental lecture on money not growing on trees. Elizabeth, as usual, didn't listen, but did ask Luke to place the bet for her to lessen the chance of criticism over unladylike appearances.

At one and a half miles, the race was a long one. Matt was concerned about Buck's ability to maintain the endurance needed for the long haul. He trained with Buck but Matt was aware that horses could act differently once pitted against others in a race, so he had no idea how the thoroughbred would run when challenged in a group.

Seven riders paid an entry fee of fifty dollars with the winner receiving one hundred and the balance going toward the new addition to the school. The race started in front of the Elkhorn and headed through town to the half-way mark then rounded a tree and ended back at the saloon.

Jack Devlin had not been seen for several days. Although Matt felt relieved, he almost wished Jack was around so he could keep an eye on him. Elizabeth took Matt's advice about not venturing out without an escort and did not go anywhere without Henry or Luke. Henry made sure she kept busy around the ranch, even letting her spend a day moving the herd to a new pasture. She was excited about this additional duty although returned home that evening sore and bruised from such a long time on a horse. She didn't dare complain, but gladly volunteered to clean stalls and tend to the garden after that.

The tension in the air was thick on race day as onlookers found a spot along the route to watch. Matt didn't want Elizabeth to stay in town. These events attracted all kinds of people and there would be many who drank too much. Fights often broke out when winnings were collected, and losers grumbled with resentment. There was always the inevitable shot fired into the air in excitement or at each other. Matt planted Elizabeth in his buggy next to Will and Margaret just outside of town near the half way marker where riders turned to head back to the finish line, leaving instructions to stay with the Spencers until he came to get her after the race. Elizabeth begged him to let her drive to the finish line, but he didn't want her anywhere near the end. Even Luke agreed that this was best, so she gave up arguing.

Griffin and Matt stood at the starting line looking over the competition. They knew most of the others and felt comfortable that Buck could beat them but a young rancher from several counties away had a quarter horse that looked promising. He was the one to beat.

"Did you rub him down this morning to loosen him up?" Griffin asked as Matt stroked the horse's head to keep him calm amidst the growing crowd.

"Yeah, he'll be fine."

"Did you double check the straps on Rachel's lighter saddle to make sure they're tight? It's not broken in yet and they can work their way loose." Griffin asked again, checking his pocket watch for the third time.

I triple checked," said Matt. He looked at the growing crowd and spotted Reece and his deputy circulating through the streets looking for anything suspicious. The sheriff had gotten additional reports about Devlin's connections in San Francisco who were known for shady dealings and didn't trust Jack to not be involved himself.

"That guy on the quarter horse is smaller than you. He'll have an advantage. Make Buck save some for the end."

"Griff, I know how to ride a horse. Been doing it longer than you. Quit acting like an old hen. He'll do fine and I won't let him break until he rounds the turn." Matt was getting anxious and Griffin wasn't helping with his constant worrying.

"We got a lot riding on this. Just want to make sure we're ready," Griffin replied as Matt climbed in the saddle.

"You're the one with everything riding on this. I didn't bet all my money on a horse race," Matt replied sternly.

"You should have," Griffin smiled. "He's gonna win."

The mayor, along with Reece, was standing on the back of a wagon so the riders and spectators could hear as he announced the participants in the race. Cheers went up when he called out the name of each rider and when Matt's name came up a thunderous roar of noise exploded as people clapped and shouted. Tom Kelly was standing with Griffin and they both beamed with pride. Men approached

Tom, shaking his hand or slapping him on the back saying they remembered Matt when he was a boy and first learning to ride. Saloon girls hung out of windows on the second floor of the Elkhorn, cheering and waving scarves. Stores closed as people lined the streets in anticipation.

Matt took a deep breath and leaned down to whisper in Buck's ear. "Stay calm, boy. Just give it all you got, and we'll be fine." He stuck his hand in his front pocket and smiled to himself when he felt the playing card. "We're ready Nuttah. I'm counting on you."

The mayor raised his gun and fired as seven horses ran hard down the street with riders lashing the reins and shouting to urge them on. Matt started in the middle of the pack but needed to move up. A cowboy on a painted horse was crowding them and it was making Buck nervous. The quarter horse was in the lead and he needed to distance himself from the others where Buck would be more comfortable.

"Come on Buck, move. Hah," Matt shouted as he slapped the reins from side to side. He could feel the horse pick up speed as he passed the paint and moved up behind the quarter horse. He tried to hold him at that pace not wanting to pass the lead horse just yet.

The road heading out of town was lined with buggies and wagons. Old men mounted on horseback speculated on who was in the lead. Couples sat on blankets watching the road and school boys climbed trees to keep an eye out from above. Elizabeth stood in the buggy searching for a sign of riders approaching. At one point she tried to stand on the seat, but the horse moved forward, and she fell. Will cautioned her to not do that again. She would have a good view of the horses as they passed without breaking her neck, if she just had patience.

Patience, however, was not one of Elizabeth's virtues. She thought she might tear her hair out if the riders did not appear soon.

There were so many people standing in her way she couldn't see a thing and finally asked Will if something happened at the start to delay the race.

"I just came from town and they were about to start."

Elizabeth was surprised when she turned around to find Jack Devlin sitting on his horse next to her. "Jack, what are you doing here? I haven't seen you since the day you came to the ranch. Luke said he safely returned your watch. I hope he told you I tried to catch up with you after you left but we must have crossed paths."

"Many thanks for caring, Elizabeth. I appreciate your efforts and apologize for any inconvenience it may have caused. I'm sure you fell behind my pace when you made the turn on Mill road. It's regrettable."

"Did you see Matt in town? How is he doing? Is he nervous?" Elizabeth was rapidly firing questions at Jack who laughed out loud as he watched her excitement.

"I'm afraid I did not see your young Mr. Kelly although I made a substantial bet on my thoroughbred, so I expect a big return, assuming the rider knows how to handle a horse in a race. Riders often get rattled when they realize they're in over their head. I'm surprised he left you unattended today."

"He didn't leave me alone. I'm with Margaret and Will. You remember the Spencers. I believe Will is helping you with investments and I wouldn't worry about Matt or Buck. He has his lucky card."

Jack looked confused by Elizabeth's answer and passed it off as a woman's silly babbling. He offered a friendly nod to the Spencers and they waved in return.

"I can't see a thing," Elizabeth said, straining to look around Jack's horse. "I wish they would all move back. I'm afraid I'll miss him when he rides by. I should have insisted on staying in town to watch."

"You better look quickly because they're coming now." Jack pointed in the direction of town as the shape of two riders in the distance grew larger.

"Can you see him?" screamed Elizabeth. She began jumping up and down in the buggy and Jack grabbed the reins, so the horse wouldn't take off as she waved her hands wildly and shouted Matt's name when the riders rode by.

Loud whistling started from down the line where Rachel and her friends were cheering. "You better win Matthew Kelly," Rachel screamed as she saw her brother round the corner and head back toward town.

The noise was deafening. Horses galloped by, kicking up dust in their wake. Men, women and children on both sides of the road were shouting and clapping, urging the riders along. Matt and the cowboy on the quarter horse were neck and neck, both fighting to take the lead.

Matt couldn't hear a thing. The faces of spectators were a blur as he approached the tree signifying the point in the road where he needed to make the turn back to town. He was shouting at Buck and watching the other rider out of the corner of his eye, not wanting to make his final move before rounding the curve. He couldn't let the other rider get too far ahead.

They were dead even coming out of the turn. Three-quarters of a mile left, and he wondered if Buck had enough left in him. He was giving it his all, but the other horse was strong. Matt glanced to the side where the onlookers were cheering and heard Rachel scream something as he flew by. Then he saw Elizabeth jumping up and down in the buggy flailing her arms and shouting. What was that woman doing? She could be killed. He left Will in charge and this is what happens. He noticed a familiar man in an even more familiar black suit holding the bridle of Elizabeth's horse and a knot in his stomach began to tighten. Jack Devlin showed up to watch the race after all. God, that guy was annoying, thought Matt. More determined than ever to win he kicked Buck's sides and slapped the reins hard.

"Hah! Come on Buck, move, move, move..."

In a flash they were gone, and the atmosphere deflated. People began to talk about the race. The couples on the hill resumed their chatter and the old men guessed at who might win. Most people were heading back to town for the celebration.

Elizabeth settled back in her seat unable to concentrate on anything but Matt and the end of the race. Bart Ferguson drove by in a wagon with Rachel and her friends.

"Where are you going?" Elizabeth called as they passed.

"Back to town to see who won. Aren't you coming?"

Elizabeth looked at Will. "Please Will, I want to be there when it's over to congratulate Matt or console him, however it turns out. I know Matt wants me to wait but everyone is headed for town and I want to go too. I can't wait to find out who won."

"Elizabeth, you know it's best to stay with us. It's for your own safety."

"I know Will, but its killing me."

"I can escort her," Jack offered. They all looked at him as if they had forgotten he was there. "I'll ride beside her and deliver her safe and sound to Matt."

"I don't like it. Matt is expecting you to stay with us and it's my responsibility. Why don't we go back to our house and wait there? I'll send a message to Matt and we can all have lunch."

"But with Jack as an escort I'll be in good hands and once Matt sees me he'll be happy." Elizabeth looked at Margaret for support but got no help. She shook her head no and looked away. I'm old enough to make my own decisions and there's no reason why I can't go to town, Elizabeth thought. A snap of the reins and the horse galloped off with Jack riding beside her on his horse, leaving Will and Margaret to follow.

Matt knew his thoroughbred was special and when the horse pinned its ears back in a challenge to the quarter horse, Matt was sure he would win. He could feel Buck beneath him pounding his hooves on the ground, driving to the finish line. He saw the Elkhorn Saloon as he turned onto the last block. Griff was standing on the wagon with Reece and the mayor. Dutch Jordan, leaning against a porch banister, stared stone-faced as he passed by in front of Miller's. Henry and Luke were crammed in with others on the sidewalk and waved him on as if they were giving him an extra push down the stretch. The quarter horse was spent. He slowed ever so slightly but enough for Buck to take the lead as Matt crossed the finish line just ahead of the other cowboy.

The town went wild. People rushed into the street cheering. Reece and his deputy fought to keep everyone out of danger of being trampled as the rest of the riders finished the race. Matt was sitting on Buck as the cowboy in his early twenties rode up beside him on the quarter horse and shook his hand.

"Congratulations on a race well run."

"The same to you," Matt answered. "Beautiful quarter horse. I haven't seen one run like that in quite a while."

"Well, you're sitting on one that runs even faster. Did you breed him yourself?"

"Won him off a gambler a while back. This is his first race, so I wasn't sure how he'd do but my brother kept pushing me to give it a try. The name's Kelly. Where you from?"

"A little place not far from Sweetwater, over on the border. My name is Josh Henson. If you ever want to sell your horse, look me up. You ran a damn good race. It was a pleasure."

"Sorry, I'm keeping this one," said Matt as he scratched Buck's ears. "If you're around later, look me up and I'll buy you a drink."

"I just might do that," said the cowboy as he dismounted and led his horse down the street to the Livery.

Griffin and Tom were the first of the crowd to reach Matt, nearly knocking him over with a bear hug as more people surrounded the three. Tom had tears in his eyes while Griff grinned like a school boy as he tossed a satisfied glance at Reece. Matt pushed his way through a group of men heading toward the wagon where the mayor stood waiting to officially pronounce him the winner.

Elizabeth was having trouble getting the buggy through the streets and made it as far as the Spencer house before deciding it would be faster to leave the buggy and walk. The closer she got to the Elkhorn, the worse the crowds were, and it was difficult to see over the heads of men who were standing in groups. If she tried to walk around them she was pushed back the way she came. She looked behind her for Jack hoping he could help navigate through the scores of onlookers, but he had disappeared. He'll catch up, she thought.

She wriggled her way to the sidewalk and could see Matt standing on the wagon shaking hands with the mayor while the audience clapped. Tom Kelly's head was barely visible over the crowd and she knew Griffin was close by. Reece drifted through the streets and caught her eye before turning to question a man leaning against a porch railing. She waved to get Matt's attention, and someone grabbed her arm.

"Hey little gal, where you going so fast?" The man pulled her toward him, holding her waist with his other hand.

"I'm headed to the wagon where the winner is standing," Elizabeth replied, trying to push away.

"Is that your man up there who won the race? I lost fifty bucks betting against him. Maybe you can help me get it back. How about a little kiss?" Elizabeth was nauseated by the smell of whiskey when the man leaned toward her and pushed back only to be knocked against him again as someone passed behind her. He dragged her down an alley, slamming her against a wall and pinning both shoulders with his hands while he kissed her neck.

"Stop, you filthy pig," Elizabeth said with disgust. She tried to push him away and moved her head to the side when he went to kiss her again. The man held her arms as she squirmed and screamed. He grabbed her face with his hand, squeezing her cheeks with such force she thought her neck might snap and glared with a sinister look.

"I don't like any man who plays a crooked card game and I don't like a man who's foolish enough to lose an animal as fine as that thoroughbred. You tell Kelly I've come for the horse. Devlin wants to pay his debts."

The man cocked his head toward the street and listened to the sound of approaching footsteps then fled down the alley in the opposite direction as Matt and Reece turned the corner with guns drawn. Griffin followed close behind.

Elizabeth ran to Matt as the sheriff and Griff pursued the man down the alley. He held her as she cried softly, still shaking with fear. Matt gently stroked her face where red marks showed finger impressions left by her assailant.

"Why didn't you stay with the Spencers?" he whispered.

"I wanted to find out if you won. I just wanted to be with you."

"But I left you with Will and Margaret, so you'd be safe. I explained how things can get after a race. You had no business coming to town by yourself."

"I wasn't by myself. I came with Jack, but we got separated in the crowd. Did you see him on the street? I'm sure he was right behind me," she cried.

Matt tightened his hold on Elizabeth at the mention of Jack's name. Once again Devlin was around when trouble began and slipped away in silence. "We've talked about this. Jack Devlin can't be trusted. Did you recognize the man who grabbed you?"

"No but he told me to tell you..." Elizabeth paused not wanting to go on. She knew this would make Jack look guilty and hesitated to put the blame on him for something he didn't do."

"Elizabeth, I need you to know what the man said. There are some things you don't know about Devlin and if he's involved you must tell me."

"He wanted me to tell you he's coming for the horse and that Jack wants to pay his debts," sniffled Elizabeth. "What does that mean? Is Jack in some sort of trouble?"

"I think Jack's in a lot of trouble, but we'll talk about this later. Right now, I want to get you home where you belong. Griff can take care of Buck and I'll tell Reece to meet us at your ranch."

It took several minutes for Elizabeth to calm down as Matt helped her in the buggy. People were meandering through town so maneuvering down the street was difficult. The two sat silent, Elizabeth with tears streaming down her cheeks and Matt sulking, not sure what to say.

"I'm disappointed you didn't do what I asked. It was my worst nightmare and it all could have been avoided," he started, once they hit open road.

"You have a right to be upset," Elizabeth explained. "I know I should have stayed and yes, I got myself into a fix, but I was excited about the race and didn't really go to town by myself. Jack was with me. I don't know how we got separated but it all worked out in the end."

"Worked out," said Matt. "You were dragged down an alley by a man who threatened you. How can you possibly think it worked out?" He took a deep breath and paused for a moment as Elizabeth's eyes welled up with tears.

"But everyone, including Rachel went back to town." Elizabeth sniffled

"Rachel is Pa's problem..."

"And I'm your problem? Is that what you're saying?" Elizabeth interrupted. She was getting angrier with every word and couldn't wait to get home. She wanted to forget everything that happened.

Matt took another deep breath. Elizabeth gave him that cold, blue-eyed stare and he knew the conversation wasn't going to end well. He hated to argue with her and regretted bringing up the subject. She was safe now and that was the important thing.

"You are not a problem and I'm sorry if that's what you think." He put his arm around her and kissed her. "I'm worried and don't want another scare like that."

"Thank you for looking for me," she replied with a slight smile.

"I'll always go looking for you." Matt sighed loudly, deep in thought before speaking again. "Maybe I should sell the horse back to Devlin and be done with it. Buck's been nothing but trouble since I got him and he's not worth you or anyone else getting hurt."

"No, please don't. You won him fairly and he belongs to you. Even though I consider Jack a friend, he has no right to badger you or threaten me if that's what you think he's done. I'd never forgive myself if you sold Buck because of this." Elizabeth squeezed Matt's hand. "Please keep him. He's Nuttah remember?"

Matt shook his head and smiled. "Elizabeth, you can convince me of anything right now." She giggled as he leaned into kiss her.

CHAPTER 15

THE BEST MEETING EVER

Matt sprang from the buggy, hitting the ground almost before the horse had completely stopped. Whistling a familiar song, he walked to the barn door, thinking of Elizabeth. It had been two days since the race when she had been dragged down an alley and threatened by an unknown man intent on pressuring Matt into turning the thoroughbred over to Devlin. It might have worked if Elizabeth hadn't talked him into keeping Buck.

Reece and Griff were not able to track down her assailant. Whether he disappeared into a nearby building or escaped on horseback, it was clear whoever was behind this scheme to take the horse was prepared to do whatever it took. Although circumstances pointed to Jack, there was no evidence he was directly tied to any of the attacks and Reece knew Devlin could not be charged with any crime based on circumstance.

Matt was angry that Devlin seemed to circumvent the law but knew Reece was right. It didn't help matters that Elizabeth was not the only woman accosted by a man after the race. There would be those who blamed alcohol or the rowdy atmosphere of the crowd and, in light of this, Reece thought it best to hold a meeting of the men in town to make them aware of the potential dangers for themselves and other women.

Will Spencer, Mr. Ferguson and Juanita Miller's husband as well as Griff, Matt and Tom Kelly planned to attend. Tom had Rachel to consider and if Matt was in danger there was no guarantee that she and Griffin were not also targets.

The garden club was preparing for their monthly meeting which was usually held in the afternoon with tea and finger sandwiches, but to ease tension from events after the race, Margaret suggested the ladies gather at the Spencer home on the same evening as the gentlemen were having their meeting at the hotel. The ladies would stay for supper and the men could escort them home afterwards.

Elizabeth spent the day chattering to Matt about the upcoming meeting set for tomorrow night. The members of the club were so welcoming since she moved to town and she felt a part of their group and for once was excited about one of Margaret's social events. When Matt left her after supper she was in a cheery mood as she stood on the porch and waved goodbye and he found himself wanting to turn around and return to her for the rest of the evening.

Matt reached the barn only to find the latch open and door ajar. Why was this left open again?" he mumbled in disgust. He pushed the door open and peered into the darkness. Horses stirred in their stalls as Matt felt the side of the wall for the nail holding a lantern while pulling a match out of his back pocket. "When I find out who keeps leaving this door open they will find my boot up their..."

Matt was drawn to sounds coming from the corral and he turned around to see horses break from their group and scatter. What's bothering them, he wondered? He pulled his gun from its holster, listening intently as he peered through the night at the shadows of animals, ears erect, huddling again. That familiar knot in his stomach tightened and he jumped at the sound of a twig snapping behind him. His hand closed tightly on the handle of his gun and he cocked the hammer with his thumb then slowly backed up to the barn, listening to his own rapid breathing. Another twig snapped, and Matt jerked his head quickly to the left in time to see a figure scramble from behind a tree and sprint toward the road. He raised his gun and aimed, following the runner in his sights.

"Matthew?"

Matt jumped again when he heard his father calling from the front door. He dropped the pistol to his side and took a deep breath before answering. "Yeah Pa, it's me."

"What's spooking the horses?" said Tom as he climbed down the porch steps and walked toward his son. "Rachel said she saw someone sneaking around out by the corral and I came out to see who it was. I guess it was just you."

"She was right, there was someone out here. I got home and found the barn door open again," said Matt as he put his gun back in the holster and reached for the lantern hanging on the wall. "I heard the horses in the corral and figured something was up and when I started to check on them, some fella caught my eye as he took off from behind that tree and headed down toward the road."

Matt struck a match and lit the lantern, holding it high in the door of the barn. "We better make sure everything's alright in here." He and Tom walked past each stall, inspecting the horses for injuries or anything unusual. Buck shook his head, moving uneasily and Matt talked softly to him while he stroked his head to keep him calm.

"There's a bridle and lead on the floor. Looks like someone may have attempted to take him out of here. I must have surprised him when I came home." He sighed deeply. "I don't know what to do, Pa.

With someone attacking Elizabeth and trying to get in this barn, I don't know how to stop it. Reece doesn't seem to help."

"You think that gambler was the one you saw running away?"

"As much as I don't care for Jack Devlin, he's not the type to do this kind of thing," said Matt. I'm not saying he's above hiring someone and I don't think he would intentionally hurt Elizabeth, but he does want this horse badly to pay off his debts. According to Reece, Richard Manning, Jack's San Francisco partner, is not someone to cross. He's gained control of Devlin's gambling house and has quite a racket going on. The White Swan was always a respectable place while Devlin was involved and had a reputation as an honest casino. Reece has been in touch with the law in San Francisco and the sheriff there thinks Devlin was swindled out of his share. Pretty amazing for a man of Jack Devlin's talents. Frankly, I'm surprised it happened and I believe he's desperate."

"And Reece says nothing can be done?"

"Devlin hasn't broken any laws. Reece can't touch him," said Matt. "It's a subject I plan to bring up tomorrow night at the meeting,"

"Sounds like someone needs to watch Devlin to see if we can't catch him in the act," said Tom. "You go on in. I'll walk down to the bunkhouse and get one of the men to keep an eye on things. I don't think Jesse will mind sleeping in the barn tonight. We aren't giving up if it means we watch that horse and Elizabeth around the clock. I know all of this has Henry worried too."

Matt pulled the latch closed and checked it twice before he and Tom walked toward the house. Exhausted, he was hoping for a good night's sleep.

"Does Elizabeth have her flowers ready for this garden club meeting tomorrow night?" asked Tom. "Rachel has spent all day potting hers in those containers Griff made."

"She's come up with something although I think she's a little self-conscious about it. She gets herself pretty worked up about these things. She didn't give a hoot about any of it when she moved here but now she's ingrained in her new life. She's become attached to Rachel and Margaret. I don't mind though because I know she has no desire to go back where she came from."

"She's a fine young lady, Matt," said Tom. "I was hoping she'd stick around. You two make quite a pair. Kind of like your mother and me."

The garden club members arrived at the Spencer home ready for a pleasant evening while their husbands met down the street in the hotel, leaving the women to talk of flowers and fertilizers and eager to taste whatever Margaret had prepared for dinner. Not only was Rachel a member, but also Bart Ferguson's mother, Edna, Juanita Miller and Mary Bernard, legendary baker of fine pastries when she wasn't making hats. It vexed Elizabeth that Clara Richter was part of the club, but she supposed it was to be expected.

Each member would bring a sample of their flowers and after presenting to the group, one woman would volunteer to lead a discussion about raising plants hardy enough for their region, producing more abundant blooms or harvesting seeds.

Matt pulled the buggy up to the gate of the Spencer home while Elizabeth sat silently with a small pot of violets she found growing by the stream on the Emerald ranch. She felt humiliated when she thought of beautiful plants grown by the others and wanted Matt to take her home, but he refused.

"These women don't care what kind of flowers you have," he said when she hesitated to get out of the buggy. "It's all about getting together and socializing. Haven't you figured that out by now? My mother and Margaret started the garden club back when there weren't many other women around. The few that were, lived on farms outside of town and these meetings were a way of sharing something nice in a territory that didn't have many nice things. When the Fergusons moved to town, it was easier for Edna to adjust to living so far away from her family and the same went for Juanita and Mary Bernard and Mrs. Richter, just as it has and will be for you. Now, I want you to walk in with your head held high, strutting into that parlor with your little purple flowers. I'm proud of you. You should never be embarrassed about anything you do."

Elizabeth gave him a faint smile and sighed. "You told me you were going up to the hills and find some wild flowers for me. Remember, little white ones?"

"I know I did," Matt said, looking guilty. "And I still plan to, but I've been busy helping Pa with things at the ranch. I promise I'll find you something by the next meeting. Just go and have a good time tonight and don't worry about the others."

He scooted Elizabeth through the door where Margaret stood greeting her guests. Matt looked at Margaret with pleading eyes hoping she would give Elizabeth encouragement and he wasn't disappointed.

"What beautiful violets," she exclaimed as she gave Elizabeth a hug. "Juanita, come look at what our wonderful young friend has brought. Have you ever seen such a vibrant color in a flower?"

"I don't believe I have," said Mrs. Miller. "It takes quite a talent to grow a good violet. I don't think I've ever known a person who can do it well. Come on in and show the others."

"They'll be green with envy," Margaret whispered as she took Elizabeth's hand and led her into the parlor where the other members gathered around a table filled with bowls of fruit and petit fours arranged on silver trays.

Elizabeth was all ears as she soaked in the advice of others during the discussion, hoping to gain their knowledge of how to improve her garden. She smiled as she thought of how far she had come since stepping off that stage months ago. She never realized how lonely she was until she moved west. People can still be lonely, even when they are surrounded by family and friends they've known all their lives. Matt was right in thinking she should be proud. No one thought her life as a rancher would last but she was proving them wrong.

"Did you bring those little violets? They grow all over the pasture behind our house. My mother says they're nothing but weeds with a little color." Elizabeth's thoughts were interrupted by Clara Richter who plopped down beside her. She tilted her head slightly as she stared at Elizabeth with a catty smile and air of importance. "I see Rachel brought her usual pansies. I brought the red roses. My father says they're so pretty they should be named after me. A rose by any other name would smell as sweet. That's what daddy always says."

"I don't think that's what the quote means," answered Elizabeth with a confused look. "And I think Rachel's pansies are pretty. She has so many colors." Elizabeth retuned a catty smile, feeling guilty that she had stooped to Clara's level. "Your roses are pretty too," she said begrudgingly.

"My mother wasn't able to come so daddy brought me," said Clara. "It's a shame they're forced to have this meeting because of your attack but I guess some women can't help attracting those kinds of men. Now the entire town is put on alert because of it. Griffin was so concerned for my safety he insisted that I not attend the race."

Elizabeth took a big breath and blew it out loudly in hopes Clara would understand how irritating she was. "Yes, I certainly understand Griff 's intentions. If you'll excuse me Clara, I need to speak with Rachel."

Elizabeth walked into the dining room where Rachel was helping Margaret with dinner preparations leaving Clara wondering about the meaning of her comments. Matt told Elizabeth in confidence that Griff had no intentions of ruining his day at the race with Clara hanging off his arm. Griffin had finally lost interest in her and unfortunately because of Mr. Richter and Tom Kelly's mutual business interests, Griff had not found a way to tactfully let Clara know and chose, instead, to avoid her.

We're just about ready," Margaret said as she straightened a glass on the table. She looked up at the sound of knocking at the door. "Elizabeth, would you mind getting that while I finish here. Will probably forgot something and sent someone to fetch it."

Elizabeth opened the heavy door to find Jack Devlin grinning with a cunning smile. "Good evening, Mrs. Rogers. It is still Mrs. Rogers, isn't it? You haven't gone and gotten married on me while I've been away?"

"Jack, what are you doing here?" said Elizabeth, startled to see him and peered around to see if anyone else was near. She had no idea how he knew she was there and wondered what he was up to. "No, I haven't gotten married and can't imagine why you would ask." She knew exactly why he had asked but refused to play his game. "How did you know we were all at the Spencer's?"

"I heard rumors of a meeting at the hotel and not wishing to participate, decided I would much rather spend my time with you lovely ladies." He turned toward the street as a wagon pulled up in front. "I've brought a surprise for the garden club. I'm sure Mrs. Spencer won't mind." Jack motioned to two men who had climbed down and were now unloading a crate. "Bring it in Gentlemen and be careful not to drop it."

"What on earth?" said Margaret as she came to the door. "Mr. Devlin, what a surprise to see you. What have you brought us?"

"Margaret, you look as lovely as ever," said Jack as he entered the foyer. "I've brought a little wine for the ladies of the garden club. I hope you will accept it with my compliments and if you will allow, I would like the honor of opening the first bottle."

Elizabeth had never seen Margaret speechless. She stood gaping for a moment as the two men carried in a small crate and waited for further instructions. Juanita Miller peeked around the corner with a curious look and motioned for some of the other ladies to come see what Jack Devlin had brought.

"Do you think it's proper to serve wine at the garden club?" Edna Ferguson whispered to Juanita Miller.

"Yes, I do," she replied. "The Spencers are one of the most respected couples in town and it's quite fashionable to serve wine at a dinner party. Mary Bernard approves, and she has attended a ball at the governor's mansion in Carson City."

"Having a gentleman attend our garden club is certainly a first," said Margaret recovering her manners. "If you've brought a plant to exhibit I believe I will faint dead away. Please, bring your gift into the dining room and, by all means, feel free to open the first bottle. We were just about to eat."

Elizabeth was spellbound as the other women cooed over Jack and giggled like school girls when he was introduced. He was charming and relished every minute. Rachel pushed her way through the gathering, practically tripping over Mary Bernard fluttering her eyes as she spoke.

"Mr. Devlin, I'm Rachel Kelly. We met at the Spencer party. Remember, we talked about your horse. I saw you at the race although I was busy and didn't have a chance to talk to you. You can sit by me."

She took his arm and led him into the dining room followed by a circle of chattering ladies who sounded like a flock of ducks waddling toward a pond. Elizabeth shook her head and smiled. Only Jack Devlin could get away with this and she was sure it would be an interesting evening.

It was the best garden club meeting the women ever attended. They were infatuated with Jack's smooth southern drawl and impeccable manners as he told stories of his antebellum days in New Orleans. He was at his best as he told jokes and flirted with the ladies, complimenting each one on their hair or eyes and comparing them to the beautiful young women he fell in love with in his youth. Elizabeth sat in amazement and laughed every time he looked her way and winked when someone would squeal with giddy pleasure at his attentions. The wine continued to flow as bottle after bottle was opened and poured.

After dinner, Margaret suggested they all move to the parlor where Clara Richter almost knocked Edna Ferguson to the ground in a race to grab a seat next to Jack. Dessert was served along with more wine and as the conversation continued, Jack rose and moved to sit at the piano in the corner. He stretched his fingers, then placed them on the keys and began to play. A collective sigh filled the room as the garden club members closed their eyes and listened.

"What a lovely sound," said Margaret. "You play beautifully."

"My mother was hoping for a violin player but there was something about the sound of Mozart on the piano that drew me to it," said Jack. "My skill is the result of many years of practice which came in handy when I got a job on a riverboat. I played my way up and down the Mississippi until I learned the game of poker. I haven't played in years. Of course, there weren't many requests for Mozart on the Orleans Belle. They demanded something a little livelier."

Jack began to play a jazz song as the women tapped their feet and swayed to the music. When he moved to livelier tunes, Juanita Miller began to sing and clap her hands. Edna Ferguson stood and danced in a circle while the rest of the ladies laughed and encouraged her to continue.

Rachel opened another bottle of wine and drank from the bottle before walking along the row of women, filling glasses as she went. Elizabeth feeling flushed and light-headed, wondered if all of this was a good idea but when Rachel decided they should dance to the lively music, she didn't hesitate to help Margaret and Edna move the furniture back to the walls or out of the room completely. Mary Bernard and Clara pulled up the rug and dragged it out to the foyer as the others partnered up for a square dance.

The guests were having quite a time. Their shoes were kicked off and hair pins pulled out as the women made themselves more comfortable with every song. Juanita took off her petticoat and threw it in the corner. Someone opened the windows when it grew too warm, allowing the music and singing to be heard for quite a distance. At one point, Mary fell as she and Clara were doing a *Do Si Do* and her dress flew up to her waist bringing a roar of laughter from everyone. Elizabeth climbed up on top of the piano and started to sing. "Allemande left with your left hand. Back to your partner for a right and left grand."

Jack Devlin played on and laughed out loud with each new dance the women tried. He had his own bottle of wine and lifted it up with a loud cheer before pouring it down his throat. Then almost fell off his chair as the ladies returned the cheer and emptied their glasses.

"I know who you are," Clara said to Jack, slurring her words and wobbling as she grabbed him around the neck.

"Of course, you do, my darling. I've spent the evening in your company," replied Jack who paused his playing long enough to loosen Clara's strangle hold.

"No, I mean I recognize you from Miller's. You were with her."

She raised a heavy arm and pointed awkwardly at Elizabeth who was chuckling as she watched Rachel and Margaret with raised dresses dancing the can-can. Jack began to play the song made famous from the dance as Clara continued.

"You were at Miller's." She began to giggle uncontrollably. "You slapped me on my... well on a most inappropriate place when I walked by. It was shocking."

"Ah, I remember it well," said Jack. "My apologies, fair lady. I meant no disrespect."

"Don't apologize, kind sir," said Clara as she wobbled away. "It was delightful."

The meeting at the hotel adjourned and men headed back to the Spencer home. Mr. Ferguson chuckled as he thought of the ladies and wondered if they might all be asleep after the stirring discussion of primrose and lavender. As they drew closer they heard the music and laughter and looked at each other in confusion.

"If I didn't know better," said Reece. "I would swear that's your sister's voice."

"I was thinking it sounds more like Elizabeth singing," said Matt.

"Swing your partner round and round. Then you throw her on the ground." The singing continued followed by a burst of laughter.

Will entered the house first and walked into the parlor followed by the others who stepped around chairs and tables as they passed through the foyer. Mr. Ferguson tripped over a rug haphazardly thrown near the door and turned with a bewildered look toward Juanita's husband. Matt and Griff stared at the sight in the parlor then looked at each other. Reece began snickering but stopped abruptly when Matt glared at him in rage. Will stood frozen in his tracks, unable to speak. He glanced at the other men and raised his voice to be heard over the laughing women.

"Margaret, what in the hell is going on here?" he shouted as the ladies one by one realized their husbands were in the room."

"Will, you're back," said Margaret as she strolled over to her husband and threw her arms around his neck. "Jack Devlin brought us wine for dinner. Did you know he played the piano? He's quite an artist."

Matt shot a look at Jack. Walking over to the piano he grabbed Elizabeth and threw her over his shoulder. "Where are your shoes?" he asked.

"In the corner some place. Put me down or I'll be sick."

"Such debauchery," grunted Mr. Miller in consternation. He grabbed Juanita's arm and dragged her from the room. "We're leaving immediately."

"Not without my best petticoat," she cried as she searched in the corner.

"You're in charge of her," Matt grumbled to Griffin and pointed to his sister who sat in the corner softly humming to herself. "Get her home to Pa."

"Griffin, where have you been? I was hoping to see you tonight." Clara stumbled across the floor, falling into Griff. "I've missed you."

"Maybe you should get Snooty Hooty home," Reece whispered to Griff. "Before her daddy gets wind of this. I can take care of Rachel if you want."

"Not on your life," answered Griff. "Mr. Richter is responsible for her." He picked up his sister and walked her out the door.

The other men were gathering their wives and heading home. Matt looked for Devlin, but he was not around. "This is unacceptable. He can't do this to decent women and get away with it," he said to no one in particular. He carried Elizabeth out of the house and placed her in the buggy then climbed in beside her and snapped the reins.

Several miles down the road Elizabeth began to moan. The ruts and the bumps weren't making it easy on her stomach. Her head was spinning, and she was nauseous.

"Matt, please stop. I'm sick."

He pulled the buggy over and helped her out, walking several steps before she bent over and began to vomit. Sitting her down on the grass, he went back to the buggy to get a handkerchief from her hand bag and a canteen of water.

"Looks like the garden club had quite a night," he said as he poured the water over the handkerchief and wiped her face.

"I know you're mad, but I didn't really drink much," Elizabeth said leaning against his chest. "We were having fun and got carried away."

"You drank enough to sit on a piano and sing like a saloon girl," Matt replied stroking her hair. Jack Devlin is a cad and I don't want you to have anymore contact with him. You belong to me."

"Even when I drink too much and get sick?" Elizabeth said with a faint chuckle.

"Especially when you drink too much, although I don't ever want to see you like this again."

When Matt pulled up at the ranch there was still a light on in the bunk house. Within minutes Henry and Luke were hurrying across the yard as they watched Matt pick Elizabeth up and head for the front door.

"What's going on here?" Henry asked. "What's happened to her? Luke, get the door for him."

"She and the rest of the ladies of the garden club had a little something extra at their meeting. Seems Jack Devlin brought wine to the party."

"Jack Devlin? What was he doing there?" Henry asked.

"Apparently causing trouble. Mark my words Henry, he'll regret this." Matt walked through the door and up the stairs to Elizabeth's bedroom followed by Luke who carried a cloth and pitcher of water.

"It'll be alright," said Henry. "She'll sleep it off. She feels better now than she will in the morning. Better give her some headache powder while she's still awake."

Matt sat by Elizabeth until she fell asleep, stroking her hair and listening to her breathe. Getting up to leave, he bent over and kissed her lightly on her head. "I love you," he whispered and turned down the light before walking out of the room.

CHAPTER 16

TWO PROPOSALS

It took everything Elizabeth had to sit up. She bent over the side of the bed with her eyes closed and head aching, feeling as if she was run over by a stampede. She cringed at the thought of the garden club meeting and what Matt must think of her. The room was still spinning as she washed her face and looked in the mirror. She groaned and threw on a robe before heading downstairs where she found Henry and Luke eating breakfast. Henry glanced up and watched as she slid into a chair, resting her head in her hands. Luke rose to fill a plate of food and set it in front of her but as the aroma filled the air, making her nauseated, she pushed it away and moaned.

"At least try the coffee," said Luke quietly. "You need something in your stomach."

She raised the cup to her lips and took a sip. It tasted bitter as she swallowed, and her face twisted as she set the cup down again.

"Think you're gonna live?" Henry asked, never looking up.

"I'd be better off if I didn't," Elizabeth whispered. "I don't remember ever feeling this bad."

"We've all felt like that at one time or another," said Luke with a sympathetic smile. "Even Henry although he's not inclined to admit it just now."

Henry shot an angry look at Luke then resumed eating. "I doubt the lady's garden club will ever be the same. Wouldn't be surprised if it was disbanded all together. If the other men were as upset as Matt, it's gonna be a long time before you women will be trusted to have a meeting."

"But that's not fair. If men drink too much at the Elkhorn they don't shut that down. In fact, men will brag about spending nights there and some are doing more than drinking," Elizabeth argued.

"It may not be fair but that's the way it is. Respectable women don't spend the evening drinking and carrying on and I shouldn't have to remind you that what takes place in a saloon is not to be discussed by young ladies. I told you from the beginning that gambler is no good. He's a bad influence on you and every decent woman in this town. I'm disappointed in you and hope I never see you like this again. You're lucky you have a man like Matt Kelly who tolerates the way you've acted."

Elizabeth was hurt by Henry's words. It brought tears to her eyes to hear him talk like this. She was too young to remember her father. Her brother had raised her and there wasn't much she could do to rile him. Of course, he was practically a kid himself. Alex demanded nothing, and her uncle spent most of his time trying to make her happy. She had grown close to Henry and Luke since coming west and now it seemed difficult to live up to their expectations. Hadn't she done everything they wanted? She worked hard to be a rancher and attended every social function Margaret pushed at her and still she felt like she failed.

"I'm sorry I'm a disappointment Henry," she said taking another sip of coffee. "Maybe Jack was wrong in showing up, but he meant no harm. Every woman there was old enough to make her own deci-sion about how to act and he certainly shouldn't be blamed for that."

"Any man who would give a case of wine to a group of women is not a gentleman and is up to no good. I blame him for this entire situa-tion and there's nothing you can say to change my mind." Henry took a last drink of coffee and slammed his cup on the table then pushed his chair back. He turned to Luke, refusing to look at Elizabeth. "I'm going out to mend that fence that's about to fall down. The one you cleared of brush. I should be back in time for lunch. You've got plenty of chores to keep you busy around here, Luke."

"Don't be so hard on her," Luke said. He squeezed Elizabeth's hand and gave her an encouraging look. "We all make mistakes and beatin' her down like this isn't gonna help."

Henry glanced at Elizabeth and grunted. "I'll be home later." He put on his hat and walked out the back door, letting it slam as he stomped down the steps and toward the barn.

"I'm going upstairs to get dressed," Elizabeth said as she rose and shuffled out of the room. "Leave the dishes. I'll clean up when I come back down." She reached the stairs and sighed deeply. If only her head would stop hurting. Grabbing the banister, she dragged herself slowly up each step, wanting to go back to bed for the rest of the day, but she was determined to get through this.

A hot bath and more coffee did wonders for her head and her attitude as she spent most of the morning working. The kitchen was clean, the floors swept, and Elizabeth sat in the rocker on the front porch enjoying the sunny day as the tree branches lazily swayed in the cool breeze blowing over the field in front of her.

Luke emerged from the barn and spotting Elizabeth sitting sol-emnly on the porch, joined her, listening to the creaking of wood as the rocker moved back and forth. "Henry doesn't mean anything when he gets in these moods," he finally said. "He was awful worried when Matt brought you home. He tossed and turned most of the night, fretting over your health and wondering if he shouldn't stay by your side in case you needed something."

"What if he's right and the garden club is disbanded," said Elizabeth after a moment.

"Don't you worry about that, Miss Elizabeth. That garden club has been around almost as long as this town. Why, Henry's wife was even a member when she lived here. That's why he fixed up that flower box for you. He knows a woman enjoys growing pretty flowers and he figured it would make this old ranch feel like home for you. Most of the members of that club have faced the threat of Indians, weather, and sometimes poverty to forge their lives in Nevada. They aren't about to let a few glasses of wine come between them and all their talk about growing their petunias. As much as their husbands may object at first, they'll be back to having their meetings before you know it. Despite what Henry says." He smiled and patted Elizabeth on the arm. "In fact, I think you should host the next meeting. You're a member in good standing and you should show the others you're not afraid to continue on the tradition."

"Even if the only thing I can grow is violets scrounged up by a stream? Clara Richter called them weeds."

"Don't you pay any attention to what that girl says," said Luke. "She hasn't a lick of sense. I bet your violets were as pretty as anything the other women brought."

Elizabeth sighed and gave Luke a half-hearted smile. He was always so encouraging and always there to lift her spirits which was especially needed today. He had become a good friend.

"Matt was supposed to go up into the hills and find some flowers for me. He said there were beautiful ones that only grew up there, but he's never done it," she said sulking. "He won't go now. He will probably never speak to me again."

"Now don't go saying those things, Miss Elizabeth. It's true he was pretty hot last night about what Jack Devlin did and I understand why he feels that way, but it'll take a lot to turn that young man away. He cares for you a great deal and he's not about to let loose of you. Now I want you to quit fretting. It's all over and there's not a thing you can do about it now. How about you and me taking a ride? I can saddle up a couple of horses and we can take a trip around the ranch. It'll take your mind off all of this."

"I'd like that. I'll go in and change into some riding pants and be ready by the time you get the horses," said Elizabeth. She ran inside, excited about Luke's offer and returned to the porch to find Jack Devlin waiting for her.

"My dear Elizabeth," he said with a bow. "How are you feeling this fine morning?"

"Like someone hit me with a brick," she replied. "In fact, I'm guessing that all of the members of the garden club are feeling this way."

"I stopped in to see Will Spencer before coming here and understand Margaret has not yet been able to raise her head from the pillow. Most unfortunate."

"You got us in a lot of trouble, Jack. Henry said the garden club might be finished. It's really upsetting," said Elizabeth with a disgruntled look.

"That's why I wanted to speak to you. I want to apologize for putting you ladies in a precarious position. I had no intentions of allowing the evening to get out of hand and don't want to see you women punished because of me," Jack said. "Although you must admit it most certainly was a lively evening," he added with a chuckle.

Elizabeth blushed and began to giggle. "It was fun, wasn't it? When Mary Bernard landed on the floor with her dress flying up I thought I would fall off the piano from laughing."

"I agree it was quite comical. I don't think I shall ever see anything like it again," laughed Jack. "At least not in this town. It's why I stopped by. I will be leaving for California this afternoon. My work here is done and since your young Mr. Kelly has refused to sell my thoroughbred back to me, I must return to my business in San Francisco. I'm afraid I've been away too long."

"This afternoon," cried Elizabeth.

"I think its best, especially under the circumstances. I will make my exit as quickly and quietly as possible," answered Jack with regret. "The time is right for me to go which is why I hoped you would consider going with me."

"Go with you?" Elizabeth said with a puzzled look. "I have a ranch to run here and a life. I'm afraid I don't have time for visiting other places now."

"It wouldn't be for just a visit," said Jack. "I was hoping you would come live with me in San Francisco. I've grown fond of you my dear and I could give you so much. You would have an exciting life of travel and parties. Whatever you wished for would be yours. Dresses, jewels, and a fine house if you so desire. You would never have to get your hands dirty again and no longer need worry about anything. We could be married right away if you want."

"Married if I want? What are you suggesting Jack?" answered Elizabeth in a perturbed voice. "I don't want to marry you and I've worked hard on my ranch and don't want to leave. I'm offended that you think you could turn my head with the promise of jewels and dresses. I guess Clara Richter was right. I'm just a country girl at heart and my heart is right here with Matt."

I figured as much," said Jack. "But I made up my mind to ask on the chance that I might persuade you."

"Is everything alright here, Miss Elizabeth?" said Luke tying the horses to a post. "Mr. Devlin, I'm afraid I'm going to have to ask you to leave. You've done enough damage to this young lady and she doesn't need the likes of you coming around here anymore."

"I was just telling her that I will be leaving town this afternoon my fine man and have just come to say my goodbyes," said Jack. He turned to Elizabeth and pulled her into his arms, leaning gently down to kiss her. "I shall always carry the memory of your beautiful face with me."

Elizabeth blushed and turned away for a moment not knowing what to say. She never realized until that moment how Jack felt. There was an awkward moment of silence as she wondered how to gracefully pull away when her eye caught sight of Matt riding up on his horse.

Seeing Jack Devlin kissing Elizabeth with his arms wrapped tightly around her waist threw Matt into a rage. His stomach turned as he dismounted and stormed to the porch where the two were standing. To see the woman he loved in the arms of another man was too much and he felt betrayed. He had his fill of Jack Devlin and this was the last time he would let this gambler interfere in his life.

He ignored Elizabeth when she started to speak and slammed his fist into Devlin's face with such force that Jack staggered back against the porch railing. "Leave her alone. Get out of town. I don't want to see you around here again," Matt snarled as Jack wiped the blood from his mouth.

"What have you done?" Elizabeth screamed. "He's a friend and has been a gentleman to me which is more than I can say for you."

Matt stood there fuming, unable to believe that Elizabeth was defending this man whom, he suspected, was behind the threat against him and had put her in danger. He was stunned by the idea that she might actually care for Jack Devlin more than him and wondered if he had misjudged her.

"What kind of a woman keeps company with a man like him? He's no gentleman and it's shameful that you allow him to kiss you," said Matt, seething.

The moment those words left his mouth he regretted them. He saw the tears in Elizabeth's eyes and wanted to take it all back. He had come to the ranch to make sure she was feeling alright after last night and to spend the evening with her and now it was ending like this.

"What kind of arrogant bully would say such a thing?" she cried. "You have no right to treat me this way and I want you to leave. I never want to see you again."

"Now Miss Elizabeth, I think you should wait a moment," said Luke trying to calm her down. "Matt is just looking out for your own good and didn't mean what he said. He's just angry now. I already told this gambler to get going and not to come back. You and Matt should go inside and take a minute to relax before anything else is said."

Elizabeth was weeping as she pushed her way passed Matt and ran toward the horses. How could the man she loved suggest she was a disgraceful woman? It was like he didn't know her at all and the time they spent together meant nothing. To hear him accuse her of wrongdoing was more than she could bear, and she wanted to run away. Everything in her life was falling apart and she didn't know how to put it back together. She untied one of the horses and hoisted herself into the saddle. Without looking back, she drove the horse hard as she galloped off toward the road.

"Elizabeth wait," Matt shouted as he ran after her, but she wasn't listening as she gave the horse a ferocious snap of the reins and disappeared leaving the three men standing motionless on the porch.

Once she felt safe from being followed, Elizabeth slowed her pace. She found herself heading north from the ranch and into the rough terrain of the hills looming ahead. Her horse needed water and she began searching for a possible source. The forbidden hills, she thought. The hills that Matt warned her about. Well, Matt was not in charge of her. He promised to bring her wild flowers that only grew in those so-called dangerous hills and since he was no longer in her life, she would take care of it herself.

The path was rough and bordered with steep rocks and her horse stumbled over the loose stones covering the narrow passage as she inched along. "What's wrong boy? What are you afraid of?" she asked as the horse pricked his ears and hesitated to move forward. He was restless, and Elizabeth looked around to see what was causing his fear. Without warning, the horse reared up, throwing her to the ground then turned and ran in the direction they had come.

Her head slammed on the hard rocks and she laid there stunned for several seconds. Finally, sitting up, she looked around, disoriented and called out for the horse in a faint voice. Her head pounded as she raised a hand to her forehead. Feeling dizzy she forced herself to stand, still calling for the horse.

Hearing a noise, Elizabeth turned toward the steep rocks and with blurry vision could barely make out the form of a cougar crouching on a large boulder above. His muscles tightened, and he growled as he glared before leaping through the air toward her. The last thing she remembered was the sound of a gun before falling to the ground and fainting.

"Matt," whispered Elizabeth when she opened her eyes to find herself cradled in his arms with the dead cougar only feet away. "How did you find me?"

It wasn't that difficult," said Matt, brushing back her hair and wiping the trickle of blood from her head. "I picked up your trail pretty quickly down by the mill road and followed the tracks to the base of the hill. I was hoping you wouldn't come this way. I told you how dangerous it was."

"I was angry and just wanted to get away. Without thinking much about it, this is where I ended up. I was going to get those wild flowers. The ones you told me about."

"I'm sorry I haven't gotten them for you," said Matt. "I'm sorry about a lot of things. Mostly about what I said earlier. Forgive me. This wouldn't have happened if I hadn't been so stupid."

"You said I was shameless as if I was some trollop from the Elkhorn," said Elizabeth.

"I know, I know," said Matt shaking his head in sad agreement. "It was wrong."

"What kind of woman keeps company with a man like that," Elizabeth mimicked in a high pitched, sassy voice, as a tear formed in the corner of her eye and ran down her cheek.

"I know, I know," answered Matt, his head nodding in accordance. "When I saw you kissing Jack Devlin I couldn't think straight. I know you said you never wanted to see me again, but I love you and I want to marry you...if you'll have me." He leaned down and kissed her, holding her close. "I'll dig up every wild flower in these hills if you just say yes."

"Yes, of course I'll marry you but only if you promise to stop shooting things. First the snake and now that cougar and even the bee on the mill road," said Elizabeth. She put her arms around Matt's neck and kissed him. "Really Matthew, we can't go anywhere without carnage falling down around us."

Matt chuckled as he helped Elizabeth to stand. "Technically I didn't shoot the bee. You're lucky I had my shotgun with me. That cougar would have been difficult to bring down with just a pistol. Now, let's get you back and have doc Larson take a look at that bump on your head."

"Where do you suppose my horse is?"

"Probably half way home by now," said Matt as he hoisted Elizabeth up on his saddle and climbed up behind her. "Don't worry, we'll find him."

"When did you know you loved me?" asked Elizabeth as she leaned her head back against Matt's chest, snuggling as much as she could against his warm body.

"When you threw that crumpled hat at me in front of Will's office."

Matt kissed Elizabeth lightly on the cheek and pulled the reins back, bringing his horse to a halt. Dismounting, he walked to the boulders where the cougar stood a short time ago and climbed up to the top. Kneeling, he began to dig into the tough dirt, and finally, pulling out a tuft of white flowers, jumped down. He handed the plant to Elizabeth with dirt clinging to the narrow roots and without speaking, mounted his horse again, gave her another kiss on the cheek and headed home.

CHAPTER 17

THE ARRIVAL OF CYRUS WALLACE

Henry stood next to Luke in front of the stage depot, pulling at the collar buttoned tightly around his neck and peered into the depot at a clock hanging behind the ticket counter. "Eleven o'clock and late as usual," he grumbled. "I don't see why we had to come meet Elizabeth's uncle when he arrives. She's getting married in three hours and seems to me like they could have picked someone else for this job. Why not Will Spencer? He's the uncle's friend and we don't even know what this man looks like. What time do you have?"

Luke nervously removed his hat and wiped his bald spot, then placing it back on his head, fidgeted with his bolo tie and leaned over to look down the road coming into town. "We're doing this as a favor to Elizabeth because Margaret has Will tied up running errands for the reception. It won't be bad. It gives us a chance to get to know him since he's staying with us while Elizabeth and Matt are in San Francisco on their honeymoon."

"We're going to have plenty of time to get to know him. Besides, if we don't take to this fellow, we're not going to want to be around him anymore than we need to," said Henry, checking the clock again.

"Here he comes. I can see the dust in the distance."

They stepped forward as the stage came to a stop in front of the wooden platform and nodded to the depot manager as he walked past on his way to open the door. An elderly gentleman, dressed in a brown striped suit and polished brown shoes climbed out and looked around.

"Mr. Wallace?" asked Henry.

"Yes, I'm Cyrus Wallace," answered the man as he stepped to the side and out of the way of other passengers exiting the stage. "Are you Mr. Turner?"

"It's Henry. This is Luke and we're here to pick you up."

Luke removed his hat and stuck out his hand. "Pleased to meet you Mr. Wallace. We're sure happy to have you here," he said timidly. "If you wait just a minute, I'll get your luggage."

"Delighted to be here myself, although this is wild country. How my niece has made it this long in a place like Nevada is a puzzle. I must say, that stage ride alone is enough to make me want to turn around and head back to St. Louis."

"She's done pretty well for herself," answered Henry, resenting the man's comments. "There's nothing to be puzzled about. Elizabeth is a fine young woman. I'm going to fetch the buggy while you two grab the luggage. Tom Kelly insisted we bring that oversized carriage he owns so there'll be plenty of room for your things."

Mr. Wallace glanced at Luke who stood anxiously eyeing the stage steps as a handsome young gentleman climbed down, followed by a young boy. The gentleman straightened the hat on the boy's head and brushed dust from his pants then looked back at the door to help a woman down.

Henry looked at Luke with a confused expression, wondering why his friend was grinning as he stared at the couple and the boy. His heart skipped a beat and he gulped loudly as tears filled his eyes and he removed his hat, crumpling the brim with his clenched hands.

"Pearl," he whispered with bated breath. "My precious Pearl."

"Papa," cried the woman as she ran to Henry, throwing her arms around him. "Papa, it's me. I've missed you so much."

Tears filled Henry's eyes as he hugged the young woman and cried out loud. "My precious Pearl, you've come back to your old papa. Luke, it's my Pearl."

"I know Henry," answered Luke as he wiped his eyes with his sleeve. "I knew she was coming and bringing her husband and boy. He sniffed loudly and wiped his face with his sleeve again.

Henry stroked his daughter's blonde hair then patted her cheeks, not daring to believe he was looking at the face of this pretty young woman whose blue eyes and soft complexion were so similar to Elizabeth's. "But how did this come about after all this time?"

"It was Mr. Wallace," answered Pearl. "He brought us here." She hugged Henry again as her husband and son stood patiently by Elizabeth's uncle.

"Actually, it was my niece's idea," said Mr. Wallace. "She wrote to me several months ago and asked me to help find your daughter. I engaged the services of a Pinkerton agent I knew during the war. A man who was once charged with guarding our late president. It was quite a challenge, but somehow, he was able to track Pearl and her husband down. When I got the news that Elizabeth was to marry, Pearl and her family agreed to travel with me to Nevada. I must say, she's a lovely girl who has married a good man."

"This is my husband, John Thompson, Papa," said Pearl. "And our son, Henry."

The boy stepped forward and shook Henry's hand. "Hello, granddad. It's nice to meet you, sir."

"Did you hear that, Luke," cried Henry as he grabbed the boy in a bear hug. "He called me granddad and his name is Henry, too."

"I heard Henry," sniffed Luke. "He's a fine lad. Miss Elizabeth is a good woman to bring Pearl out here. I can't believe your girl is standing right in front of us."

"How long can you stay?" asked Henry, looking at Pearl's husband. "There's no need for a hotel. We've got plenty of room at the ranch and Elizabeth won't mind. I hope it won't inconvenience you, Mr. Wallace. They can stay in the bunk house with me and Luke, so we won't put you out."

"Once again, my niece has taken care of everything," answered Cyrus. "She and her new husband will want to go into more details, but I plan to stay with my friends, Will and Margaret Spencer, at least until Elizabeth returns from San Francisco, so you and your family will have full run of the ranch. Margaret is finishing preparations for the move to the little house in town where Pearl, John and Henry will live until the new home is built on the Emerald."

"New home? Little house? I don't understand," said Henry, looking around at the others. "What do Elizabeth and Margaret have up their sleeves now?"

Cyrus cleared his throat and smiled as Pearl grabbed her father's arm and kissed his cheek. "We're here to stay Papa. Mr. Spencer, who we've never even met, has offered John a position as an accountant in his business. We're so blessed."

Henry looked at Cyrus Wallace and then at Luke, unable to speak. He put his arm around his daughter while still holding his grandson tightly with the other arm. "An accountant," he said as if spellbound. "Luke, how about that? An accountant."

"I know, Henry. Miss Elizabeth and Margaret have been planning this for some time. Those two found a little house in town where Pearl and her family are going to live until Matt and Elizabeth build a brand, new house on the land Tom is giving them. When that house is finished, Pearl and her family are going to come live with us at the ranch."

"What does your mother think about all of this?" Henry asked Pearl.

"Mama died three years ago, Papa," answered Pearl as she dabbed her eyes with a handkerchief. "She never stopped loving you, but she couldn't bring herself to move back to Nevada after what happened to Mae. Her last words were of you."

"I'm afraid we may have given away more than we should, Henry," said Cyrus. "We'll let Elizabeth and Matt fill you in on the rest. Now, if it's alright with all of you, I'd like to see my niece and this young man who has stolen her heart."

⚓

Matt stood nervously at the front of the church shifting from one foot to the other, rubbing his sweaty palms on his pant legs. He licked his lips and tried to remember the name of the song floating from the organ pipes. Something Elizabeth wanted, he thought, or maybe Rachel. He couldn't recall.

"I've got a horse tied up at the back door and fifty bucks in my pocket that's yours if you want to slip out quietly," said Griffin out of the side of his mouth. "No one will blame you."

"Are you mad?" whispered Matt. "Why would I want to walk out on the most wonderful woman I've ever known and the best thing I've ever done? You can't possibly know how I feel."

"Jeez, it was just a joke," said Griff, rolling his eyes. "If this is love I want no part of it. I think you've taken leave of your senses. Not that Elizabeth isn't a great girl. Too good for the likes of you. You haven't been the same since you met her. I miss the old you sometimes."

"You miss me?" said Matt. "Talk about taking leave of your senses."

"You know what I mean," said Griff. "I've got no one to argue with now or play cards or go hunting."

"Well, I'm not dying for crying out loud," said Matt, flashing a tentative smile at Margaret as she and Will sat down next to his father and brother, Lance. "You act like you'll never see me again. Besides, you've still got Lance and Reece to get in trouble with. That won't be hard for you three and I'll be around to play some cards on Saturday night."

"Again, with the lost senses," said Griff in a low voice. "Do you think Elizabeth is going to let you go to the Elkhorn with us and play cards? She'll have you washing dishes and sweeping floors once you move into that big house you're building. Your fun days are over."

"My fun days are just beginning, Griff," answered Matt, nodding at Henry when he entered the church. "You wait, your days of domestic home life are coming, and you won't think a thing of washing dishes." He spied Clara Richer waving from the front row. "Looks like Clara is willing anytime you give her the word."

"Now who's gone mad," grumbled Griff, avoiding Clara's eyes.

"We're ready, Matt." The preacher nodded to Mary Bernard who was sitting at the organ. She momentarily stopped playing, and then started again with a different song as Rachel started down the aisle toward the front of the church.

Seconds later, Elizabeth emerged from the back holding on to her uncle's arm. Rachel insisted that Elizabeth wear Eleanor Kelly's wedding gown and she was stunning. The garden club members created a beautiful bouquet made of flowers gathered from each member's garden and she held them tightly as she moved down the aisle, smiling at Matt.

"Eleanor would have loved Elizabeth," blubbered Tom. "I'm so proud to have her as part of the family."

"I think she must be looking down at us on this day," said Margaret, comforting him.

After the ceremony the couple and their guests moved to the Spencer home where Margaret had prepared a wedding feast like none the town had ever seen. The cake was cut, musicians arrived, and the celebration began, lasting late into the evening. Matt couldn't stop smiling as he held onto his bride's hand and mingled with their friends.

Elizabeth was happier than she had ever been in her life and hugged Pearl when Henry introduced them. "Thank you for bringing Papa and me together again," Pearl said.

"You've made an old man happy," Henry added. "I'll never forget this."

"I love you Henry," Elizabeth said as she kissed his cheek. "I'll miss you when we're gone."

"We're only going for two weeks. We need to leave soon because I'd like to spend a little time alone with you tonight and we have a long ride on the stage tomorrow."

"Before you go, Matt," said Henry, pulling him to the side. "I want to thank you for all you've done and letting me and Luke stay on to run the ranch."

"I would sell it to you outright Henry, but Elizabeth can't let it go. Not yet at least. You and Luke are doing me a favor by keeping it going. Besides, Elizabeth would never forgive me if I didn't let you live with Pearl and her family since they've moved here for good. Now, if you excuse me, it's time for me and my bride to leave while the night is still young, if you know what I mean." Matt winked at Henry as Elizabeth was pulled from Margaret's grasp while Rachel stood crying. She threw her bouquet into the crowd as single girls fought to catch it, and then drove away in a flurry of waves and goodbyes.

CHAPTER 18

A Bargain for Life

Elizabeth jumped from the buggy and ran to Luke, throwing her arms around him in a big hug. "I missed you." she said. "Wait until you see what Matt gave me." She pulled the gold locket from around her neck. "See, it has the letter K on the front with our wedding date engraved on the back and our pictures are inside."

"That's very pretty, Miss Elizabeth. I told you he was a good man," said Luke, admiring the necklace. I bet you two had a good time in San Francisco."

"It was wonderful. We went on a fishing boat and saw a whale. It was huge. I've never seen anything like it."

"Surprisingly, they don't have a lot of whales back in St. Louis," said Matt with a chuckle as he unloaded a trunk from the buggy and set it on the porch. "Elizabeth loved the ocean so much we spent about every day eating lunch by the docks."

"It was beautiful, Luke. Where's Henry?"

"He took the wagon to the mill to pick up some fence posts he's having cut. He's still not happy with that piece of fence we cleared off and is determined to tear it down and start again. He should be back soon if he doesn't decide to go to town to visit with little Henry. Those two are becoming pretty good friends. Want some help with that trunk, Matt?"

"I got it, I think," said Matt, heading for the door. "Let's get inside. Elizabeth is dying to show you everything she's bought."

Luke chuckled as he followed the two in, watching Elizabeth throw open the lid and rummage through clothes all the while talking excitedly about their trip. "Was she like this the entire trip?"

"She was like a wide-eyed kid wanting to see and do everything. I'm not sure she can go back to boring old ranch life."

"She'll calm down now that you're home," said Luke. "Once you get that new house built, Margaret will keep her busy with decorating. I hope you didn't spend all your money in San Francisco."

"I've saved a few dollars. Are you working around here today? I was hoping to run an errand."

"Henry told me not to move a step until you two showed up. What did you need me to do?"

"I was thinking about going to town to order a new branding iron. We've decided to name our new ranch the Circle K," answered Matt. "What do you think of that idea?"

"I think its fine, but what's Tom going to say?" asked Luke

"Pa and I talked about it before we left for San Francisco. He understands that my share of the Emerald belongs to me and Elizabeth now. We'll raise our family on the land just like he and my mother did."

"Matt, there's something I think you should know. It has Henry worried and me too," said Luke.

"Some fella by the name of Richard Manning has been asking around town about you and that race horse of yours. Reece questioned Dutch Jordan, seeing how Dutch is mixed up with that gambler and his crooked friends. Dutch admitted that Manning is Jack

Devlin's business partner and owns part of the White Swan gambling house in San Francisco and he's come here looking for Buck and Devlin too. Manning has threatened to kill Devlin. None of us care much for Jack Devlin but I think you'll agree we don't want to see him killed."

"No, I don't want to see him harmed. I just want him out of our life. I thought I ran him off the last time he showed up here," said Matt. "What's Reece doing about this?"

"Reece is keeping an eye out for him and has already told Dutch he would be arrested if he knows where Manning is and doesn't tell the law. No one's seen Devlin since you two got married. Reece figures he's left town for good and probably hiding out some place, so Manning doesn't find him. That's another reason why Henry wanted me to stick around here today until you got back."

An anxious frown replaced Matt's smile. Once again, he wished he'd sold Buck to Devlin. The safety of his family was worth more than a horse or anything else for that matter and he's tired of having to look over his shoulder. Maybe Richard Manning showing up wasn't such a bad thing. Perhaps he could strike a deal with him and be done with it.

"Are you alright staying here with Elizabeth while I go into town to talk to Reece?" Matt asked. "I want to find out the whole story and see what we need to do to find Manning. I agree with you that Jack Devlin is probably on the run."

"I don't mind at all," said Luke. "You know I'll do anything for Miss Elizabeth. Besides, Henry should be back soon. You go on and take care of what you need."

"I'll be back as soon as I can. Do me a favor and don't mention any of this to Elizabeth. She's been so happy to be home that I don't want her worried."

"I won't say a word," said Luke. "She'll want to show me all those pretty things you bought her. That should keep her busy for a couple of hours."

⋏

Elizabeth walked to the barn, still tired from the stage ride home, but anxious to see Buck. She was annoyed with Matt for going back to town, so he appeased her by promising to take her for a ride when he returned. Only men could be excited about a new branding iron, she thought. Opening the door, she found Buck safe in his stall and stroked his nose as he nuzzled against her.

"Did you miss me, boy?" Elizabeth picked up a brush and began to groom him. "Are you ready to go for a ride later to see where your new home will be? Matt is going to build you a pretty new stable with lots of room."

Hearing the squeaky hinges of the door move behind her, Elizabeth turned, expecting to find Luke. "Did you groom Buck at all when we were gone? He looks a bit matted."

"Luke's not gonna answer any time soon after that hit he took on his head. In fact, I think he's gonna be out for quite a while."

Elizabeth gasped when she saw a man pointing a gun. "What do you want? My husband will be back any minute." She backed up, partially hiding behind Buck.

"My name is Richard Manning and what I want is standing next to you. Jack Devlin made a big mistake when he lost that horse to Kelly. I'm disappointed in his ability to come away from a card game with my treasured prize. Now I'm forced to take back what belongs to me."

"This is our horse. Matt won him fairly and I believe Jack would admit to that. You have no right to be here."

"Jack Devlin is a dead man. He owes me a debt and the horse is payment. I've warned our friend many times about crossing me and now he's run out of chances," said Manning. He pointed to a nearby saddle. "Be a good girl now and saddle the horse for me."

Elizabeth was shaking as she threw the blanket and saddle on the horse. When she finished, the man took the reins and motioned for her to walk out the door. She was panicked and trying to think of something to do to stall, hoping Matt would return. She got to the door and grabbed a pitch fork leaning against the wall and throwing it at the man, turned and ran for the house. She hadn't taken five steps before Manning grabbed her by the neck and threw her down.

"Get up and don't try anything like that again. I can shoot you here just as easily as I can down the road. Now we're gonna get on the horse."

He mounted Buck and pulled Elizabeth up to sit in front of him. "Where do you plan to take us?" she said, looking around for Luke as they rode off. She hoped he would recover quickly from whatever wound Richard Manning had inflicted on him.

"I'm going back to California. This horse is destined to have a long career on a race track just as I'm destined to rake in the profits. Once I'm sure we're cleared of this place, you, I'm afraid, will meet your untimely death."

"My husband will find me first and he won't give up until you're behind bars. Everyone knows Buck belongs to us and you can't hide him or yourself in California or anywhere else for that matter."

Crossing through the pastures of the ranch and on to Emerald land, Manning avoided running into another traveler until he emerged on the main road north of town heading for the state line. A mile down the road they came upon a young cowboy headed in the direction they had just come.

"There's a rider up ahead. You keep your mouth shut and let me talk. I've got my gun pointed at your back and I won't hesitate to use it on both of you if you don't do what I tell you."

Elizabeth cringed as she felt the hard muzzle of the gun press into her back. She looked around desperately for a way to escape but believed Manning's threat to kill her and the approaching rider if she didn't do what he said. She bit her lip as she took a deep breath, intently watching as the rider drew closer.

"Afternoon," said the cowboy with a curious look as he tipped his hat and smiled. "You folks out for a ride on this pretty morning?" The cowboy looked at Elizabeth as she dropped her eyes to avoid his stare. She sat stiffly in the saddle barely breathing as she waited for the young man to pass.

"Yes, I was taking my wife on a picnic." Manning gave Elizabeth a peck on her cheek and she shrunk from his touch. He poked her in the back with his gun to show his displeasure. "Isn't that right sugarplum?"

"Yes," Elizabeth replied without looking up. "We're going on a picnic."

The cowboy didn't take his eyes off Elizabeth as he continued. "That's a beautiful horse you have. You don't see many like him in these parts. How long have you had him?"

"Not long. I bought the horse for my wife. That's why I'm taking her for a ride," Manning replied uneasily. He was annoyed with the cowboy for asking too many questions. He knew the longer they delayed, the more of a risk there was of being discovered by Matt Kelly or the sheriff and he wanted to keep moving.

"That's a pretty locket you're wearing ma'am. Is the K your initial?"

Elizabeth could feel the gun in her back and sensed the tension in Manning's voice. She knew if she couldn't find a way to end this conversation her life and the life of this young man would end here. She struggled to stay calm and played with the gold locked around her neck.

"My name is Kathryn," she blurted out, looking up with pleading eyes. "Kathryn with a *K*. It's a gift from my husband. Now, if you will excuse us, we're anxious to be on our way."

"Yes ma'am, you have a good day." The cowboy tipped his hat again and continued down the road. He knew there was something wrong. Two people going on a picnic without a basket of food didn't make sense. The woman was scared, and her frightened look said it all. He wondered if, with all his questions, he might have pushed too hard and put the lady's life in more danger than he suspected she was already in. The cowboy might not have noticed had it not been for the buckskin horse. It was the same thoroughbred he raced against the last time he came to this town. The one owned by a man named Kelly who said he would never sell the horse. He quickened his pace and stopped by the sheriff's office as soon as he got to town.

Matt was talking with Reece when the cowboy walked in. They recognized each other immediately and Matt rose to shake his hand.

"I didn't know if you would remember me from the race," said the cowboy. "The name's Josh Henson from over by Sweetwater. Are you here about your stolen thoroughbred?"

"My horse isn't stolen. He's safely tucked away in the barn on my ranch," said Matt, confused about why the cowboy would think Buck was gone.

"What can I do for you?" said Reece, with a suspicious look. Even if Matt was acquainted with this cowboy, considering all the strangers coming to town looking for Buck, Reece wasn't in a trusting mood.

"I just saw Mr. Kelly's horse about five miles north of town, heading west. A man and his wife were riding him," answered Henson.

"Things didn't seem right. His wife was too scared to say a word. Seemed odd to me and since the last time Kelly and I spoke, he said he would never sell that buckskin, I thought I ought to report it."

"Are you sure it was my horse?" said Matt. His curiosity was peaked and his mind racing about what could have happened at the ranch. He wondered if Elizabeth talked Luke into taking Buck for a ride before he got back.

"I rode neck and neck with you for over a mile and I swear that was your thoroughbred."

"What was his name?" asked Reece who glanced at Matt. "What did they look like?"

"Didn't tell me his name," said Henson, "He was probably early forties with dark hair. His wife was a pretty woman with blonde hair and blue eyes. She wore a gold locket with a letter *K* engraved on the front. She said her husband gave it to her."

"Elizabeth" Matt shouted, turning pale. "It's Devlin and he's got Elizabeth. Can you show us where they were?"

"Sure, but no telling how far they've gotten by now," said Henson as he followed the two out. "They have a big head start on us."

The three mounted up, racing north with the cowboy in the lead. Matt was crazy thinking of Elizabeth and what Jack Devlin might do to her. He was stunned that Jack would hurt her and livid with Luke for letting this happen."

"You're going to have to stop soon and rest the horse. He can't continue carrying both of us," Elizabeth said stalling for time. Matt should be back at the ranch by now and would be looking for her. She had to find a reason to slow their pace.

"He'll be fine. We need to keep moving if I'm going to cross the border before that guy back at your ranch comes to."

"You certainly don't take very good care of Buck considering all you've done to get him. He won't be worth much if you wear him down like a pack horse. My husband would never let him go this long without a rest."

Exasperated, Manning promised to stop for water if they spotted a concealed place on the way but made no attempt to look. He continued on, more concerned with a place to dump Elizabeth. The cowboy had already seen them, and he wasn't taking the chance of running into someone else. There was cover up ahead by a grove of trees and a stream to water the horse, so he headed in that direction. Nearby cliffs posed the perfect place to get rid of her. By the time someone found her it would be too late.

"Get down and don't move," said Manning as he lifted Elizabeth off and dropped her to the ground. He dismounted and led the horse to the stream while she glanced around looking for a place to escape. Manning had a gun, so it would do no good to run unless she could make it to the cliffs behind them while his back was turned. If she could get out of range of his gun she might maneuver around and hide from him, in hopes that Matt or Henry may have figured out where they were headed. At least it would be better than waiting here like an animal unknowingly being led to slaughter.

Manning stood by the water's edge holding Buck's lead while he drank. Elizabeth took a deep breath and for a moment thought of Alex and her brother Jim. Would her life be cut short as theirs were? The image of Matt filled her mind and she could almost feel his arms around her and she wished for one last opportunity to tell him how much she loved him. Lifting her dress, she took off toward the steep rocks.

"Stop, you foolish girl," shouted Manning, seeing her run out of the corner of his eye. "I told you to stay put." He pulled his gun from its holster and aimed.

Oh God, let me get to the cliffs, thought Elizabeth. If I can just reach the edge I might have a chance. The image of Matt was still on her mind as her feet dug into the ground, pushing her closer to her goal with every step.

A shot rang out causing her to shudder, but Elizabeth did not turn around. Manning must have missed, she thought. I'm still alive. She reached the bottom of the cliffs and heard another shot, wondering if Manning was chasing her and if he was gaining ground. Her hands grabbed the rough surface of a large rock and she pulled herself up and over, moving higher when she spotted a man standing above. Elizabeth was startled as she watched him point his gun and fire over her head. One more blast of a gun from behind and the man above grabbed his arm in pain. Jack Devlin settled on the rocks, looking down at her.

"Well, Mrs. Rogers," he yelled. "We meet again."

Elizabeth was speechless. She stared as the sleeve of Jack's white linen suit reddened with blood, and then turned around to find Richard Manning dead on the ground. "Jack, are you alright? What are you doing here?" She started to climb the steep cliff again. "You shot Manning," Elizabeth called out in breathless gasps, sitting down beside Jack when she reached the top.

"I did, indeed, fair lady," answered Jack, wincing. "And with much pleasure, I might add."

Elizabeth helped him remove his jacket and tore the shirt away from his arm to inspect the bullet wound. It doesn't look bad. I think you're just grazed." She lifted her dress and ripped the bottom ruffle from her petticoat, gingerly wrapping it around Jack's wound.

"Ah, my dear Mrs. Rogers. If I should die right here on the spot, it will be with the memory of your sweet petticoat wrapped lovingly around me."

"Stop it," Elizabeth said, annoyed at Devlin's comment. "You're not going to die and it's not Mrs. Rogers anymore. I am now Mrs. Kelly and please do not talk about my petticoat."

"Oh, I see your young Mr. Kelly is as lucky in love as he is in cards," said Jack, smiling. "You know, gamblers liken the queen of hearts to the beautiful Venus. She's known as trustworthy and faithful and we believe she must be kept in our life at all cost. It did not escape me that your brave knight picked up the queen from the discard pile the night of that fateful game. I should have known then that you would never be mine."

"Really?" Elizabeth said with an inquisitive look. "He told me he traded the queen of hearts in for a lucky seven, but it still worked out for us."

"He may have traded the card, but he kept the queen in his life all the same. However, you still have time to change your mind. We can escape together. I would give up gambling and resume my export trade on the coast."

"I told you before, I love Matt, but giving up gambling for a respectable job might be a good idea, considering you almost got us killed over a horse."

The sound of horses from behind them made both turn. It was Matt and Reece, followed by the cowboy. Elizabeth knew he would come for her and she stood waving to him. "Elizabeth," Matt shouted as he jumped down from his horse and ran to the rocks. Spotting Jack, he pulled his gun and aimed. "Don't move or I'll shoot. Elizabeth, climb down to me. You're safe now."

Reece knelt over the body of Richard Manning, searching for a pulse. "Who the heck is this guy?"

"That's my old partner, sheriff," called Jack. "Mrs. Kelly will confirm he was killed in self-defense."

Elizabeth helped Jack stand and guided him as they climbed down the steep cliff. "He saved my life. Manning was going to kill me and take Buck," she said as she reached Matt and threw her arms around him. "Put your gun away, Matthew. I warned you about shooting things when we go places."

Matt glanced at Devlin, embarrassed. "What was I to think? Besides, I wasn't going to shoot him. I just wanted to back him away from you." He kissed her, and then held her close. "Are you alright?"

"I'm fine, although a little shaken. Who's that with you and Reece?"

"Josh Henson. He was one of the other riders in the Elkhorn race and recognized Buck when he passed you on the road. If it hadn't been for him, we wouldn't have known where you were," said Matt. "What's Jack Devlin doing out here? Was he part of this scheme to get Buck?"

"It was all by chance," said Jack. "I've tried to watch out for Elizabeth since I discovered Manning was after the horse. Dutch Jordan was charged with keeping track of you. He followed you two home from the church bazaar. That was him she saw lurking around her bedroom window."

"Who was shooting at us after the Spencer party?" said Matt, not believing Jack's story. "You left early so how do you explain that? What about the day you went to her ranch? Who was following her on the mill road?"

"I admit it doesn't look good," said Jack shrugging his shoulders. "I left the party early because I suspected Dutch might try something stupid. Unfortunately, I was searching for him in town while he was waiting for you on the road. I visited Elizabeth at her ranch to make sure she was safe. Once again, I was concerned she might be in danger. When I left that afternoon, I ran into Dutch who was on his way to try to recover the horse. I watched from afar as Elizabeth headed for town in the wagon and turn down the road toward the mill. I followed until she got stuck. Dutch was up ahead waiting for her and you, as it turned out and I rode ahead to shoo him off."

"I never did trust Dutch," said Reece. "Was he the one sneaking around the barn on the Emerald ranch?"

"No, I believe that was the crusty pirate who attacked Elizabeth in town. I stayed with her that day of the race and when she insisted on going back to find you, I knew I needed to tag along but I lost her in the crowd," said Jack taking Elizabeth's hand. "I'm sorry I didn't do a better job of protecting you, but you were too sly. I had no idea Manning sent one of his goons until after the incident was over."

"I wish you would have said something Jack," said Elizabeth. "I never would have left your side."

"That still doesn't explain how you got out here today?" said Reece. "Seems like more than a coincidence you happened to be waiting here when your partner showed up with Elizabeth."

"Imagine my concern when I learned Richard was in town. I knew he wouldn't give a second thought to killing me. Dutch said as much. I went to her ranch only to find Luke out cold. After bringing him around and finding out my partner had taken the horse along with this lovely lady, I headed for the only place I thought he might go which, of course, was back to California. One man on a horse travels faster than two people and I must have passed Manning and Elizabeth somewhere. I arrived here moments before they did and waited for my chance to capture him and save your beautiful wife. The best thing she could have done was run toward the cliffs. It drew him out in the open where I could get a better shot."

"You know I'm going to have to take you in, Devlin." said Reece. "There will be a hearing over Manning's death and I suspect a few conspiracy charges since you were aware of the attempts on Matt and Elizabeth's lives."

"No," cried Elizabeth. "He saved me, and we have to save him. I'll say I was the one that killed Manning and shot Jack." She turned to Matt with tears in her eyes. "Please, don't let this happen."

"You want to let him off to go back to California and resume his life with no consequences for what he's done? How can you suggest such a thing?" Matt was hurt that Elizabeth still held Devlin in such high regards after everything he confessed.

"You won't have to worry about me resuming my former life," said Jack with a beaten look. "When the rest of Manning's men find out he's dead and I'm still alive they will pursue me to the ends of the earth. I won't live to see San Francisco again, once you take me back to town and I end up in jail."

"Matt, please." Elizabeth threw her arms around him and cried. "I couldn't stand to see that happen."

"It's not my decision," said Matt comforting her. "Reece is the sheriff and he has to uphold the law as he sees fit."

"That's right," said Reece with a disgusted look. "Make me look like the bad guy. What do you expect me to do?"

"How about arresting Dutch Jordan? You can say I was the one that killed Manning and let this has-been gambler go. That is, of course, assuming I never have to see him or hear the name Jack Devlin again. I don't mind taking the blame." Matt kissed Elizabeth and smiled. "Would that make you happy?"

"You're worse than her," said Reece, shaking his head. "Now you want to make a dishonest sheriff out of me."

"Not, dishonest, Reece," said Elizabeth, letting go of Matt and hugging Reece. "You'd be a kind, reasonable man who sees the situation as it really is."

Reece took a deep breath and walked away for a moment, deep in thought as he stared at the dead body of Richard Manning then turned back toward his friend.

"No one ever hears a thing about this. Not a peep or I'll haul all three of you in for conspiracy. As far as anyone knows, Jack Devlin was killed by Manning and his body never found. Understand? And

I want your first born child named after me as payment for all of this."

Elizabeth ran to Reece and hugged him again. "Thank you, I knew you were a good man and I'll never forget you. Neither will little Reece, if we ever have a boy."

"Nor I, my good man," said Jack, bowing deeply. "If I should ever have a son, he too will be called Reece in honor of your distinguished gesture."

"Take your horse and go, Devlin, and as Matt said, I never want to see your face around these parts again," grumbled Reece. He looked at Richard Manning lying on the ground and moaned. "Somebody better help me get this body back to town. I'm not doing all the work."

Josh Henson stepped forward and grabbed Manning's legs. "We can throw him over my horse and I'll ride that thoroughbred back. It will give me a chance to see how he runs."

"Why did you happen to be headed this way this morning?" asked Matt. "Talk about a coincidence."

"I came to see you. First, to collect that drink you promised and second to make you a proposal."

"Proposal?" said Matt

The cowboy smiled and looked at Buck who was still standing by the stream. "Ever since that race I've been thinking about your thoroughbred and wondered if I might borrow him as a stud. I've got a mare that's got some speed and I wondered what kind of foal they would produce."

Matt looked at Henson, surprised at the idea. He hadn't thought of breeding Buck until now. Josh helped save Elizabeth's life and he certainly felt he owed the cowboy a favor. He could let Josh take the first foal and Matt would take the second. Subsequent foals would be sold. "Why don't you follow us back to the ranch and we'll talk more about it over that drink. Reece won't mind taking Manning back to town by himself."

Reece groaned as he helped Josh Henson pick up Manning's body."Not a word from any of you about this and I want one of those foals. I think I'll name it Reece, seeing how I'm such a kind and reasonable person" he said sarcastically. "Get going Devlin before I change my mind."

EPILOGUE

Matt pulled on the reins, bringing the wagon to a halt. Climbing down, he grabbed a box from the back and bounded the porch steps to where Elizabeth sat, rocking a baby. He knelt and kissed them both, then took the little girl's tiny hand in his. "How are my two favorite girls, today?"

"Cranky, but nothing a long nap won't fix," said Elizabeth stroking the baby's blonde hair. "She was almost asleep before you pulled up."

"Little Hope's mama thinks she's cranky," said Matt kissing the tiny fingers he was holding. "I don't believe it." He picked the baby up and strolled back and forth on the porch, cooing to the little girl as he walked.

"Do you think Reece is disappointed we didn't have a boy to name after him?" asked Elizabeth as she watched the baby laugh and reach out for Matt.

"Nah, he's got his colt and that's good enough for him," answered Matt. "Besides, there's nothing to say we won't give Hope a little brother one of these days."

"I think Reece should be happy with the horse as payment for our bargain. Have you forgotten how disappointed Griff was when

Reece got our first foal and he didn't? I don't think I could look your father or brothers in the eye if we started naming children after the sheriff. People might begin to talk."

Matt laughed and bent down to kiss Elizabeth. "I have no plans to name our child after anyone but family. We've already decided to name a son Jim, after your brother and I've promised Griff the next foal even if I have to pay Josh Henson for his share. I think that's enough debt payment for us."

"What's in the package?" asked Elizabeth, pointing to the box sitting by the steps. "Something for the house, I hope."

Matt scooted the box toward her with his foot as he nibbled on Hope's fingers, making her laugh and then hiccup. He searched his pocket and pulled out a penknife, handing it to Elizabeth. "It's got your name on it, so I thought it was something you and Margaret ordered. It doesn't have a return address."

Elizabeth opened the knife, slitting the string wrapped tightly around the box and slowly pulled the flaps back. Inside, was a round, pink and white striped hat box and she looked at Matt inquisitively. "Are you sure this was addressed to me? I haven't ordered anything."

"It's addressed to you," repeated Matt. "The stationmaster waved me down when I drove by to let me know it came in on the stage. Open it up and see what it is. Maybe Rachel bought you a gift. You know she likes to do that."

Elizabeth removed the string and tugged at the top of the box. She pushed back the paper stuffed inside and lifted out a straw hat decorated with blue ribbons. Smiling, she placed it on her head. "Are you sure you didn't buy this for me?"

"I'm positive," answered Matt. "I'm telling you, it was probably Rachel. Why are you looking at me so funny?"

"This is just like the hat I wore the day I came to town. The one that got smashed by that awful man on the stage and the one I threw at you in front of Will's office," said Elizabeth, tying the ribbons under her chin. "Don't you remember?"

"I guess it does look a little like that hat. Maybe Rachel thought you would like a replacement."

Elizabeth emptied the box of paper and pulled a picture from the bottom. She laughed as she ran her fingers over the photograph then held it up for Matt to see. "It's a riverboat," she said, looking at Matt's puzzled face and waiting for a reaction. "The Orleans Belle. That's Jack's boat. The one he worked on when he was young."

"So, the hat is from him?" said Matt. "Is there a letter to go with it?"

"No just the hat and the picture."

"Well, I guess this proves Jack Devlin hasn't changed his ways," said Matt. "Even when he's given a second chance."

"You don't know that," answered Elizabeth. "Jack told me his first job on the Orleans Belle was as a piano player. Long before he became a gambler. He really is quite talented. Maybe if he's taken up an old profession again, it's playing the piano and not poker."

"Elizabeth," said Matt, shaking his head. "You can never bring yourself to see the real Jack Devlin."

"Maybe not," answered Elizabeth, with a nostalgic look as she stared at the picture. "But I can't help thinking there's more to Jack than the sly gambler with a deck of cards and a bottle of whiskey, content with his nomadic lifestyle. I want to believe he will have a better life and find happiness like us. There's always that hope."

"That's why I love you, Elizabeth," said Matt. "And why I love our own little Hope." He leaned his head toward the girl who reached out and grabbed his hair, causing him to yelp. Pulling her hand back, he laughed. "You are just like your mama, my sweet baby. You have her smile and beautiful blue eyes and I got a feeling, you're going to be a handful. But it'll be worth every minute, just to watch you grow up."

Matt took Elizabeth's hand and pulled her from the chair. Putting his arm around her, they started for the door. Pausing for a moment he kissed her then guided her into the house. "What do you say we put this baby to bed and work on a little brother?"

"Matthew," Elizabeth said, blushing.

"Pa's going to want a grandson," said Matt as they walked up the stairs. "And I kind of promised Griff..."

"Promised Griff what?"

"About that name we had picked out for a boy..."

The End

ACKNOWLEDGEMENTS

Many thanks to my family and friends. Your shared suggestions, time, support and love helped me write a better story and follow a dream. I love you all.

About the Author

Leigh Stephens has a passion for reading and writing. For years, she expressed her creativity through her work in the newspaper industry as well as entertaining friends and family with stories. She is a native of Rock Island, Illinois and graduated with a degree in Communications from Western Illinois University. She lives in Rogers, Arkansas, with her husband. They have two children and a grandson.

www.ingramcontent.com/pod-product-compliance
Lightning Source LLC
Chambersburg PA
CBHW070836120626
46556CB00002B/774